THE SPO...
COMING ...

"Captain Hilton!"

The volume was deafening, close to pain level. Jim clapped his hands over his ears, wincing from the roaring voice, booming and unrecognizable, battering the senses.

"Captain Hilton and the crew of the *Aquila!* Anyone know about Operation Tempest? Show yourselves." The Chinook was about two hundred yards away, to the north of the ghost town, hovering over a maze of dry ravines.

"Sorry we're a day late on the rendezvous here... tech problems. Come on out, folks. Okay, we got you on the scanners."

Now the blinding light had located them, sucking them into a cone of brightness so powerful it almost felt like being suffocated in a force field.

Jim Hilton held his breath, feeling like a fly trapped in amber. He was aware of Sly Romero screaming in terror.

Then above it all, the noise of gunfire.

EARTH BLOOD

JAMES AXLER

Deep Trek

A GOLD EAGLE BOOK FROM

WORLDWIDE ®

TORONTO • NEW YORK • LONDON
AMSTERDAM • PARIS • SYDNEY • HAMBURG
STOCKHOLM • ATHENS • TOKYO • MILAN
MADRID • WARSAW • BUDAPEST • AUCKLAND

This one is for Mary Engesser who's been riding
shotgun for a lot of long days' journeys into light.
We've never met, yet, but we share some good
memories of a good friend. This comes with my thanks.

First edition March 1994

ISBN 0-373-63808-6

DEEP TREK

"The sudden explosion of a handgun, the hiss of razored steel, the scream of a hunting creature, the earthquake's rumble . . . these are some of the most frightening noises in the world. But nothing can compare to the terrifying sound of total, utter silence."

—From "The Dragon Dies" by
Tony Hills, Cymru Press, 1990.

PART I

PART 1

PROLOGUE

Captain James Hilton, lately the commander of the United States Space Vessel *Aquila,* stared down the sunlit main street of the abandoned ghost town of Calico, California.

There was the dazzle of the chromed hood of the sleek silver Mercedes sports car parked near the open front of what had once been a popular gift shop. Mica wind chimes still tinkled in the light breeze, and he could just taste the faint, elusive flavor of piñon pine candles.

There were five bullet holes in the car, not counting the smashed windshield. The nearside fender was crumpled and smeared with brown, drying blood. One of the double headlights was gone, and Jim could still make out the macabre hank of blond-haired scalp that dangled from the socket.

The rough surface of the old picnic table in front of him felt warm to the touch. He glanced at the sky, seeing it was cloudless from east to west.

It was November 15, 2040, the date and the place that Zelig had warned them to attend.

He looked around, seeing what changes the past seven eventful weeks had wrought in his command. Mentally he ticked off the names of the crew, finding to his dismay that some of the faces had already blurred.

Dr. Bob Rogers from Topeka, dead in his cryocapsule.

Mike Man, the best chess player that Jim had ever known, dead in the landing crash.

Marcey Cortling, the Aquila's number two, decapitated.

Ryan O'Keefe, their psychiatrist, also dead at Stevenson Base.

Jed Herne, shot by a sniper not far from San Francisco, his death described to them all by Jeff Thomas that morning.

Pete Turner and Henderson "Mac" McGill, both missing, believed killed. Their planned trip up to New England had been the longest and the most dangerous. Mac's loss was about the hardest to bear of the seven dead or lost.

Then there were the survivors from the *Aquila*.

Himself.

Steve Romero and Kyle Lynch, who'd left together and returned together.

Jeff Thomas, beating the odds to return to Calico.

And Carrie Princip, who'd been such a vital support for Jim through the past seven weeks.

Down to seven from twelve.

But they also had some additions.

Hilton's own daughter, Heather, eleven years old. She was sitting on the porch of what used to be the house of the town's schoolteacher, playing a game with a handful of quartz pebbles along with ever-smiling Sly Romero. The boy was about eighteen, but he acted more like ten. His round, gentle face turned toward Jim, and the boy waved a soft hand.

Jim waved back, then turned his head to the north, where the ground rose steeply, close by the remains of an old mining railway. He felt the woman before he saw her, conscious of the intensity of her gaze.

The enigmatic Nanci Simms, immaculate in her khaki pantsuit and polished boots, stood on the ridge and stared at him.

There were some questions there. Jeff had come in with the sixty-year-old stranger, but he hadn't talked much about her. Jim Hilton reckoned the questions could wait awhile.

There was no sign of Zelig, no sign of anyone moving as far as the eye could see. Just the ocher expanse of the desert, stretching away, unchanged and eternal. But the dried shards of sagebrush and mesquite still showed in the distance, carrying the scarlet tint of the lethal plant cancer that had ravaged Earth while the *Aquila* was on its mission. It had caused the deaths of tens of millions of the planet's population, changing life forever.

Jim sighed. "What now?" he said.

1

The pile of paper advertised the Barstow Film Festival: February 1st Thru 10th, 2040.

Jim Hilton browsed quickly through the list of vids and movies that were scheduled. A few names he recognized, and a few more he didn't. A retrospective season of Peckinpah's best, as well as a new print of the cult classic *Repo Man*, including six minutes of never-shown footage and a rare candid interview with the director, an eighty-five-year-old Englishman called Alex Cox. He was also the guest of honor at the festival.

The other side of the flyer was clear, except for a few lines about a special late addition: The Best There Ever Was—The Films of Harry Dean Stanton.

"Him I've heard of," muttered Jim.

It had occurred to him that some sort of a log or a journal might not be a bad idea, something to set down a record for anyone coming after. There was a pencil in the desk, and he took one of the sheets of dry, dusty paper and began to write.

THE UNITED STATES Space Vessel *Aquila,* under his command, had been out on a two-year deep-dark mission. When the crew had been brought back out of cryosleep prior to landing, it had been to find a changed world, a world ravaged by the plant cancer known as "Earthblood," which had destroyed all plant life across the planet in a matter of months.

When the plants died, the animals and birds and fish died. And then the people.

Cities were boneyards where only ghouls now lived. Towns were abandoned to the flourishing scavengers like the coyotes and the vultures.

Small communities either vanished or became armed camps of gun-hungry vigilantes.

I went up to my old house in Hollywood with Carrie Princip. She was second navigator on the *Aquila*. Found my wife and one of my twin girls dead. Brought Heather back here to Calico.

Jim reached for a new piece of paper, wondering idly if the Barstow Film Festival had ever taken place, guessing that the ecodisaster would have struck too quickly.

Steve Romero and Kyle Lynch went off together, up to Colorado. Steve was the radio honcho. Kyle, the only black in the crew, was chief navigator. They came back safely with Steve's boy, Sly. Nice kid, with Down's syndrome.

That covered six of the eight.

Outside, through the shattered glass of a side window, Jim could see Jeff Thomas walking with Nanci Simms. The *West American* had paid millions of dollars to get their star journalist on board the mission. Now Jeff had the greatest scoop in history but no newspaper to write for. No newspapers anywhere, except for the ragged pages that were blowing in the wind.

Jeff had gone out toward San Francisco along with Jed Herne, the ship's electronics expert. Jed had also played free safety for the New York Giants before a bad knee injury finished his career.

Now he was dead, shot by a sniper.

That was what Jeff Thomas had told Jim Hilton when he arrived in the old ghost town.

Jim wrote, "Jed Herne, killed on the way to San Francisco. By rifleman." Then he drew a question mark and circled it.

Jefferson Lee Thomas. After the disastrous crash landing of the *Aquila* back in Nevada at Stevenson, he'd weighed a pudgy one-sixty-five. Now he'd slimmed down to around one-fifty.

Arrogant and argumentative, he'd not been the most popular crew member, but now there was something different about the twenty-four-year-old. Something at the corners of his eyes when he'd been telling Jim and the other survivors about the murder of Jed Herne.

"Heard the crack, then Jed went down. Clean through the head. Didn't say a word. Never saw the man who shot him. One moment he's walking along with me, then he's flat on his back, staring up at the sun with sightless eyes."

Only problem was, Jim had heard him telling Steve Romero that they'd both been on mountain bikes and that the killer had been a raggedy old man with white hair.

He thoughtfully circled the question mark again with the blunt stub of pencil.

The last name was Nanci Simms.

Though she was open and pleasant and obviously extremely tough and resilient, she had an oddly guarded, impenetrable quality.

She looked to be close to sixty, though her six-foot body was in terrific shape. Jim Hilton had shaken hands with her and he had felt steel and whipcord in the grip. Jeff had introduced her as a retired schoolteacher from San Francisco.

Jim hadn't met many retired lady teachers who carried a 16-round, 9 mm Port Royale machine pistol across their shoulders and a pair of Heckler & Koch P-111 pistols on the hip. Greased and ready for action.

He shook his head.

The light was just beginning to fade away toward the west as the sun dipped behind the Sierras. Night came fast out in the desert. The fifteenth day of the eleventh month of the year was nearly over.

There'd been no sign of General John Kennedy Zelig. He'd been the senior officer in charge of the space mission. Now, with something mysterious called Operation Tempest, Zelig had left them a runic message to all meet together in the ghost town of Calico on November 15.

They were all there, the survivors, but nothing had happened.

Just the eight of them. He wondered what had happened to the other couple of crew members who'd survived the crash and the bloody attack on them back at Stevenson Base.

Henderson McGill and Pete Turner. Mac was the astrophysicist and, at forty-five, the oldest member of the *Aquila*'s complement. He'd also been Jim Hilton's best friend. Pete had been second pilot, a thirty-six-year-old widower with no children. His wife had been murdered by muggers, years earlier, on the Lower East Side of New York. An expert in martial arts, Jim had reckoned Pete had a better chance than most at making it.

Mac and Pete had headed northeast, on much the longest odyssey of anyone. With no family, Pete Turner had been happy to travel with Mac, who had been married twice and had seven kids. One wife, Jeanne, lived up on Mount Vernon Street, in Boston. And Angel, the second Mrs. McGill, had a Victorian Gothic white frame house on Melville Avenue in Mystic, Connecticut. Jim knew the house, having visited it several times over the years.

But with winter closing in, there had always been a risk that the snows would catch them—if some other grinning death hadn't gotten to them first.

They hadn't come back.

Jim knew Mac. If he hadn't returned to Calico for the agreed date, then something serious had stopped him. Something like no longer being alive.

Jim laid down the pencil, looking at the neatly written notes.

Out of the window he could see Nanci Simms leaning against the wall of what had once been the ice-cream parlor.

Jeff was in front of her, and it looked as if they were having an argument. The journalist, half a head shorter than the woman, was shaking his finger at her, pointing behind him toward the rest of the township. Jim realized that they had no idea that they were being watched.

He looked away from them, whistling tunelessly between his teeth, glancing again at his notes and deciding that it hadn't been a good idea after all. He scrunched up the brittle sheets of paper and dropped them to the splintered boards of the floor.

"What's the point?" he asked himself. He stood up, stretching, hardly aware now of the thirty-five ounces of revolver on his right hip.

It was a GPF-555 Ruger Blackhawk Hunter. Six-shot, .44 caliber, full-metal jacket. Blued steel with cushioned grips and walnut inserts.

Jim had already lost certain count of how many people he'd killed with the gun.

Out of the open door he saw his daughter, walking slowly and wearily toward him, dragging her feet through the red-gold dust.

Behind him he heard the sound of a squeal of shock or pain, quickly muffled.

Before he turned to look, Heather called out to him. "Hi, Daddy!"

"Hi, kitten." He grinned, instantly remembering. "Sorry. Forgot. Hi, Heather."

Behind him came another strange yelping sound. Jim still didn't glance around.

"I'm real tired, Dad."

"Me, too. Best wait until full dark in case Zelig delivers on his message."

The girl stood about fifteen yards away, scrawling with her toe in the rutted dirt. As the night came racing in, the temperature dropped like an iron bucket down a well. Jim could see the pale ghost of his daughter's breath, frosting around her pursed lips.

"Can I go to bed?"

"Sure. They got the fire going good?"

"Yeah."

"Be with you in a minute."

The girl waved a casual hand and turned, walking back rather more briskly through the gloaming. Jim Hilton could catch the aromatic smell of burning logs from down the street.

At last he looked behind him, through the broken window, and saw a strange tableau.

Though the light was diminished, he could make out Nanci Simms bending forward a little. One hand was locked in Jeff Thomas's bushy hair. His face, already badly scarred from the *Aquila*'s crash, was distorted with pain. The woman was forcing him slowly to his knees, talking to him softly all the time and smiling at him.

Jim stood, silently watching. He saw the ex-journalist groveling in the dirt, head lowered, Nanci pressing him down until his mouth was against the polished black leather of her boots. Kissing and licking them.

It seemed to Jim that Jeff wasn't really struggling all that hard to get away.

NANCI HAD BROUGHT plenty of food, crammed into the trunk of the damaged Mercedes.

As they ate by the fire, she glanced over at Jim Hilton. "You know Jeff and I had that unfortunate tangle on the way here?"

"Sure."

"Cops," interrupted Jeff.

"Let me tell it," she said quickly. The man leaned back as though she'd slapped him. "*Looked* like cops. Might have been highway patrol—" she hesitated "—once. Not now. I was thinking they might get some friends and track us up here, Jim."

"You reckon?"

Far away in the deeps of the diamond-starred night, they all heard a lone coyote howling at the sliver of moon that showed itself behind a wrack of thin, high cloud.

"I think it's not beyond the realm of possibility," she said.

Jim thought that she surely sounded like a schoolteacher. Then he thought about Jeff Thomas crawling in the dirt. And about the heavy weaponry she carried.

"Post guards?"

"You're the man in charge, Jim," Nanci replied with what he felt was a touch of barely contained sarcasm.

"Then we will."

The rest of them stayed silent, their attention on the food.

After the meal Kyle Lynch walked over to join him. "Thinking about Mac and Pete?" he asked.

"Yeah. Figure they both must have taken that last train to the coast. Still, guess you never know. Maybe..."

He stopped as both of them heard the unmistakable sound coming toward them from the north and west. Toward Bakersfield or maybe where Fresno had once been.

The unmistakable sound of a helicopter.

2

The battery-powered clock on the table by the barred window was showing three minutes to midnight, on November 15.

Henderson McGill had got up to go to the washroom, pausing on his way back to bed to stand in the living room and stare out across the white expanse of the rear garden. Part of the fortification of his second wife's home, in Mystic, had involved the radical cutting back of the Earthblood-blighted trees and bushes, creating an open area down to the stone wall at the bottom of the large plot.

Three-quarter-inch iron bars had been cemented into the frames of all of the windows on the first floor, preventing any would-be intruder from forcing an entry.

Mac gripped the cold metal, setting his jaw. It was almost impossible for him to come to terms with what had happened . . . what was happening.

Seven weeks ago he'd still been shrouded in a deep cryosleep, plunging dizzily through the whispering abyss of black space, locked away into the dreamless darkness.

From that first waking moment, it had been like living through an endless nightmare. A barren wilderness road where the markers were corpses.

His knuckles whitened, and he rested his forehead against the cool iron. Closing his eyes, he found himself sinking into a stupid and pointless prayer that all of this would really be only a chimera of the night, that he would open his eyes again and all would be well.

"Can't sleep, lover?"

Mac sighed, aware of the bitter cold that made his breath fog the glass near his mouth. "Yeah, Angel. Just thinking how well you all did to stay alive in the middle of..." He let go the bars and gestured toward the snow-covered garden. "The middle of all this madness. This death."

She came up behind him, putting her arms around him, her breasts pressing insistently into his back. "Look on the bright side, Mac. We got guns and supplies. Folks around here...those still living...know we're the McGill fortress. Not likely they'll make a play against us. We sit out the winter here."

"Then?"

"What you said about Zelig and the messages. Could mean that there's some sort of place set up somewhere. We could go find them."

"Today was the day for the meet at Calico." He took another long slow breath, laying his hands on top of his wife's. "Wonder how it went, how many got there, what they found?"

Angel laid her head against his back, squeezing him more tightly. "No way we'll find that out, not for some time. Snow always closed in hard over New England, and there are no ploughs out on the freeways tonight, lover."

Her hands moved a little lower, from around the muscular walls of his stomach, then lower still.

"Hey," he whispered.

"Jeanne doesn't mind it. She and me talked about this."

Mac could feel himself responding to her touch. He felt a moment of shock at the realization that it had been over two years since he'd last had any sort of sexual relief.

"Better go into the bedroom before I go off half-cocked."

"Feels like more than half to me, lover. Lot more."

IT WAS eleven minutes after two o'clock in the morning.

McGill rolled silently from his bed, managing not to disturb his wife, who was sleeping contentedly on her back. Her mouth was half-open, and she was snoring gently.

He washed quickly in the blue-and-white porcelain bowl that had come from England nearly two hundred years ago, wincing at the touch of icy water. The bowl had been carried by his great-great-great grandmother as they fled the oppression of the Highland Clearances to seek their fortunes in a new land across the gray waters of the Atlantic.

On its soft, rounded shape were faded pictures of old flowers with forgotten names.

The night was passing and the frame house was settling, its beams accommodating to the bitter chill of the darkness outside.

Mac stood again and stared across what had once been a shady and pleasant garden. It had now become a cleared firezone with good lines of fire running from side to side and no dead zones to shelter crawling enemies.

Behind him the iron-framed piano still stood against the wall. The moonlight gave enough of a glow for him to be able to read the title of the sheet music that stood open—a song from the middle part of the previous century, called "Daydream Believer." It had always been one of the favorites of his daughter Pamela.

He resisted the temptation to tap out the melody and hum the words about the reality of life that confronts the homecoming queen.

There was a photograph on top of the piano, and Mac leaned forward to look carefully at it. It had been taken nearly three years ago on a bright summer afternoon, smiling eyes gazing toward the time-set camera.

The clouds feathered away from the edges of the moon, and the room became brighter. Somehow it seemed to make it colder, and Mac, only wearing a cutoff pair of stone-washed jeans, shivered.

He picked up the picture, remembering the moment as he wiped a smear of dust from it.

John had been around seventeen. The stubble of his first beard glowed gold in the photo like an inverted halo.

Paul, a year younger, had his hands folded in his lap. Mac had noticed too late that the boy was giving the finger to the camera.

Pamela had bangs back then, a fringe of hair dangling over the veiled brown eyes. A hint of a smile lifted the corners of her mouth. Was that because she'd started to secretly see Dermot, the local leader of the pack?

He angled the picture, realizing with a shake of the head how like her mother, Jeanne, his oldest daughter was.

The background had puzzled him for a few moments, his memory blurring on him. Now he saw it was a patch of cropped turf near the tumbling waters of the Ottauquechee, not far from White River Junction, up in Vermont.

A long, deep gorge, the rocky walls smothered in mosses and lichens. A long green cavern. Now he guessed that it would all be tainted with the Earth-blood crimson, dead and barren under the covering of snow.

Quechee Gorge. Helen had been just six years old when the two families got together for one of their regular picnics. She'd misheard the name of the place and had insisted on calling it "Greasy George." It was a saying that entered the annals of the McGill tribe.

Jocelyn and Jack were standing on either side of Angel, who was waving a mock-angry hand at being photographed. Little Sukie, still in diapers, was sitting on her lap, pudgy fist in her mouth, eyes rolled back as though the clouds were the most interesting things in the entire universe.

Mac slowly and carefully replaced the picture on top of the old rosewood piano. That had been in the long-gone days of 2037, immeasurably far away now. The only good thing about it was that they were all still alive, and together.

The big man moved again to look out at the side gardens of Melville Avenue, Mystic.

Paul and John had flattened the fence between their property and the Cordells' on the left side. Jeanne had told him how their neighbors had vanished a day after the National Guard had closed the highways and never returned.

There was an empty lot on the opposite side. There had once been a small Unitarian chapel there, but it had burned down in the late 1990s and never been rebuilt.

In the sinking moonlight the ground sloped away toward a small brook. Beulah Creek, narrow in summer and frozen over in winter. Beyond that was the dark mass of Howell's Coppice, the woods stretching for about fifteen acres, mainly overgrown spruce and a few oaks.

Now it was a maze of dead trees, the stark stumps standing jagged and clawed like tumbled monoliths in an ancient graveyard.

Mac turned away, wondering again about Jim Hilton and the others, getting solace from the security of the house.

BEHIND MAC, unseen among the coniferous cemetery, a cluster of dark shadows squatted. Eyes glinted in the moonlight, watching the fortress-home.

One of them, taller than the rest, made a beckoning gesture.

"God smiles on us, brethren."

"Hallelujah, Preacher Casey," came the ragged, pattered response.

"Jesus wishes us to go forth and slay the greedy unbelievers."

"Amen, Preacher, amen to that."

An ax blade, chipped and scored, shone silver among the dead trees. "They that have shall have not. They that take shall give, yea, to the last drop of their evil blood."

"And we get the woman, Casey," growled a deep voice.

"Sure we do, Brother Glass."

"When shall the butchering begin, Preacher?"

The elongated, tattered figure turned and grinned. "What's wrong with now, brethren?"

3

Nanci Simms was at Jim Hilton's shoulder, right hand shading her eyes against the moonlight that shimmered over the rocky desert to the far north of Calico.

"Chopper, coming in low and fast," he said.

"Old Chinook. Half speed. Don't know what kind of fuel they're using, but it doesn't sound like top-quality aviation spirit, does it?"

"You sure it's a Chinook? Last time I saw one it was in a museum near Anaheim."

"Yeah. Started building the old Vertol 114 about eighty years ago. Six hundred saw service in Nam. One of them brought out nearly two hundred refugees in a single hop."

He looked at the blur of her face. "How come you know so much, Nanci?"

"Hobby. Like the War Between the States. Because I'm a woman, Jim, doesn't mean that I have to spend all of my resting moments lying on a chaise lounge and embroidering roses and lilies on sanitary pads. Does it?"

He was glad that it was too dark for the acid-tongued woman to see him blushing. "Sorry, Nanci," he mumbled.

"Old Chinook. Two free-turbine turboshafts. Sixty-foot rotors and fifty-foot fuselage. Well, fifty-one feet if you want to be pedantic, Jim. Maximum speed just under two hundred miles an hour. Want the rest of the specs?"

"No. No, thanks."

"Who is it, Dad?" asked Heather, standing at his side in a cotton T-shirt and trainers.

"Could be the good guys," he said.

"Zelig?" That was Steve Romero, with his son, Sly, holding his arm.

"Might be."

Nanci Simms whistled softly between her teeth. Jim Hilton had already noticed that she was somehow fully dressed and armed. The Port Royale machine pistol was in her left hand, the matched pair of Heckler & Koch P-111 automatics on each hip.

"Everyone for a hundred miles around'll have heard them coming in." It was almost as if she was talking to herself.

"Meaning what, Nanci?"

"Meaning that I hope they got a good ground lookout ahead of them."

"The fake cops?" Jeff Thomas was one of the last to join the watchers.

"Very good, Jefferson," she said sarcastically. "Your memory is getting better."

"Think they might try and attack them?" Jim paused, struck by an afterthought. "Or us?"

A part of him wondered why he was deferring to Nanci Simms. What did a sixty-year-old teacher know about combat? Then again, what did a thirty-three-year-old United States space commander know about combat? Not a lot, he concluded.

"Going away," said Sly in a booming voice. "Big noise going away."

Everyone listened intently. Carrie Princip broke the silence. "Damned if he's not right. Sound's going to the east."

"Good boy," said Steve, patting the big teenager on the shoulder.

"Yeah, Dad, me heard it going away, the big, big noise."

"Coming in on a figure-eight recon pattern," said Nanci Simms.

"Who do you think it is?" Jim asked her.

"Know about the same as you do, Captain. You could engrave our joint knowledge on the head of a pin and still have room for an angelic host."

"Swinging back again," said Kyle Lynch. "Look, you can see its navigation lights."

"Stupid bastards," hissed Nanci with a sudden, surprising venom. "Why aren't they playing 'Hail

to the Chief' and letting off fireworks? If I was..."
She allowed the sentence to trail off into the California night.

"How do we know they're on our side?" asked Heather Hilton.

"We don't. But it makes most sense, after the messages for us to be here in Calico. They're heading away toward the west now."

Kyle Lynch looked around them. "Think we ought to try and show some lights for them to land? Some rough terrain here."

Jim nodded. "Good idea. Could use the Mercedes for a start."

"Don't think that's a good idea, Jim."

Somehow the woman's interruption wasn't a surprise. "Why's that, Nanci?" he asked, managing to keep a tight rein on his anger.

"They've got infrared night scopes on the Chinook. Been standard for ten or twenty years now. Also we don't want to bring in anyone else who might be waiting and watching out there."

"You're paranoid, lady," said Carrie Princip. "You reckon there's black hats behind every cactus?"

Nanci turned slowly, smiling with perfect teeth at the younger woman. "I'm not paranoid, doctor. They *really* are out to get me. That was the old joke, Second Navigator Princip. Funny joke, in the old times. Sort of joke your parents might have found profoundly amusing—once.''

''What do you know about my parents?''

''Nothing. Semi wiped them away a couple of years or so ago. Silver wedding anniversary, was it not, Carrie?'' A measured pause. ''Not too far from Yellowstone, I believe.''

''How the fuck d'you know?''

''Obscenities in the mouth of a woman are as maggots within the heart of a rose.''

Carrie insisted, ignoring the gathering rumble as the chopper made another diagonal turn and came swooping in low toward them. ''I asked how you know about my parents? How could you know?''

The light blue eyes seemed to reflect the moonlight like silvered contact lenses. Jim was watching Nanci and he saw the way her lips tightened.

''Jeff told me.''

Carrie spun around, staring at the journalist. ''Did you?''

''What?''

''Tell her?''

Jeff shook his head, blinking, rubbing his eyes. ''Sorry, Carrie, I didn't...''

Nanci held her hand on his arm. ''I was telling Carrie that you had recounted the dismal saga of her parents' untimely ending, Jeff.''

"You were..." The wheels and gears moved slowly and meshed. "Oh, yeah. Sure. I told Nanci about it, Carrie."

"Getting closer," said Sly.

The helicopter was jinking from side to side, the Doppler effect of its engines bouncing off the shadowed walls of the arroyos around the ghost town, making it difficult to judge how far away the chopper actually was. But it certainly seemed to be drawing nearer.

"If there are any hostiles out there," began Steve Romero hesitantly, "the chopper should be able to pick them up. Don't they have night scopes and heat seekers on board?"

Jim answered him, getting in before Nanci. "Sure. But if it's Zelig, they'll likely be concentrating on finding us."

A searchlight suddenly stabbed into the darkness, like a spear of dazzling whiteness. Everyone blinked and tried to shade their eyes.

"Fireworks, Dad," said Sly, hugging himself excitedly.

"Anyone hiding out there with even a Kentucky musket could bring them down," said Nanci to nobody in particular. "They have to be very confident. Or just dumb."

There was a loud hissing, crackling sound, as though a speaker had been switched on.

"They have missiles?" Jim asked.

"Sure. Some kind of SRAMs most likely. An AGM-74F? Something like that. Bigger missile like the old Maverick? Could be a pair of Dirty Harrys. The Mark 10s? Sure, they got plenty of power. But attacking from the ground to a chopper is much like shooting fish in a barrel. As I've said, either they're confident and they're sweeping as they go, or they are seriously dumb."

The crackling grew louder as the Chinook came lower, close enough for them all to feel the dusty downdraft from the twin blades. Sly covered his eyes and cried out in alarm, but Steve put his arm around the boy, reassuring him.

The spotlight was cutting toward them, faltering over the buildings at the top of the hill by the old mine workings.

"Captain Hilton!!" The volume was deafening, close to pain level.

"Shit!" Jim clapped his hands over his ears, wincing from the roaring voice. Booming and unrecognizable, it battered the senses.

"Captain Hilton and the crew of the *Aquila*!" Someone on board the chopper must have realized that they were too loud. The thunder diminished. "Anyone there in Calico? Anyone knows about Operation Tempest? Show yourselves."

Now the voice was recognizably human and certainly unlike General John Kennedy Zelig's strange, thin little tones. This was a robust man, whose voice had what sounded like an Idaho twang to it.

The Chinook was about two hundred yards away, to the north of the ghost town, hovering over a maze of dry ravines.

"Why don't they come right in?" yelled Jeff Thomas at the top of his voice, then added barely audibly, "If they know we're here."

Nobody bothered to answer him.

"This is transport from Operation Tempest. We know the *Aquila* made it down and we know there were several nonsurvivors. Sorry we're a day late on the rendezvous here. Tech problems. Come on out, folks. We can... Okay, we got you on the scanners. Stay there and watch the dust. Coming in."

Now the blinding light had located them, sucking them into a cone of brightness so powerful it almost felt like being trapped in a force field.

Jim Hilton held his breath, feeling like a fly trapped in amber. He was aware of Sly Romero screaming in terror.

Then, above it all came the noise of gunfire.

4

Henderson McGill was on his way back up the wide staircase, fingers brushing lightly against the balustrade, when he was startled by the jagged sound of breaking glass.

It came from the front room downstairs, which overlooked Melville Avenue, and the noise repeated from the kitchen. Someone yelled out in the darkness.

Then wood splintered as if someone was throwing a jimmy hard against the back door.

"Attack!" shouted Mac at the top of his voice. "We're being attacked!"

More glass shattered, this time in the side room, where they stored most of the emergency food. He turned his head, listening, trying like an animal to work out how many were out there. Had to be half a dozen. Probably a lot more, judging by the yelping.

Paul was first out on the landing, holding a 12-gauge pump action in his left hand, wearing a pair of jeans and a T-shirt.

"Get yourself a gun, Dad," he said, voice as calm as if he was suggesting putting more catsup on a toasted bun.

John was at the top of the stairs, his muscular body a pale blur in the darkness. "Don't anyone touch the lights," he called. "Little ones stay put. You all know what to do."

Now both of the women were out of their rooms, with seventeen-year-old Pamela at their heels. All of them held identical .32-caliber automatics, SIG-Sauer P-230s, each with eight rounds. They ignored Mac, who was still standing on the stairs. Jeanne pushed past him and crouched at the bottom, while Angel went beyond her, stopping at the end of the hallway to kneel by the door through to the kitchen. Both of them kept silent. Pamela followed John toward the stairs to the third floor, where the attic windows would give a good field of fire out around the house on all sides.

Paul was still on the landing, checking that everyone was doing what they should be doing, going where they should be going. The noise from below and out in the watery moonlight was louder—more glass and breaking wood.

"Dad?" he said quietly.

"Yeah. Shit, these bastards, son."

"Just go get a scattergun from our bedroom. They're all loaded and ready to use." His voice became sharper. "Don't freeze on me, Dad. Either do it right now or go with the little ones. You're in the fucking way, standing there."

The snap of anger got through to Henderson McGill, and he nodded. "Sure, I hear you."

He was up the stairs and into his sons' room, seeing the gun cabinet against the wall. He'd built the shelves himself, over there, opposite the window, to accommodate Helen's extensive and hideous collection of Gerty the Goat models, in all of the clattering shades of fluorescent purples and pinks. Now it was just wall-to-wall weaponry.

Above him there was the vibrating boom of guns opening fire on their attackers and a choking scream from the garden.

There was enough light for him to make out a row of Winchester pump-action shotguns, 12-gauge, 8-round, Defender 1700 models.

But the first weapon that came to his hand was his own scattergun. Mac had bought it in Boston around the time, seven or eight years ago, when he'd first started taking the two oldest boys duck shooting up in the Adirondacks.

It was an imported shotgun, from Italy. As he took it down, the blued-steel weapon felt just right, like using a familiar razor to shave. A 16-gauge pump action, it held only five rounds.

It was made by Luco Brazzi & Sons of Genoa. His fingers brushed over their engraved trademark on the receiver—a man's head, with curly hair, eyes closed, surrounded by a number of lethal, elegant pike.

Mac had promised himself a second-hand English Purdey for his fiftieth birthday and had even got a separate account in the First National. He'd been halfway to the fifty-five thousand dollars it was likely to cost him. Maybe more with inflation.

"Not now," he whispered to himself. "Not now and not ever."

Clutching the weapon to his chest, Mac realized with a start that he'd been letting his mind wander. All around him there was a chaos of shooting and yelling. The harsh smell of cordite drifted into his nostrils.

The house was suffering a serious attack, and the family was in danger.

His house and *his* family.

"Right," he said, levering one under the hammer. "Right."

FOR ONE HEART-STOPPING, hideous moment, Mac nearly pulled the trigger on his children. His nerves were stretched so tight that the unexpected flurry of movement as he ran into the small dark bedroom made him jump.

Helen sat on the bed in a dressing gown, holding Sukie on her lap. Jocelyn and Jack were on either side of her. Helen had a chromed .22-caliber revolver on the blanket by her leg and she grabbed at it as her father appeared.

"Wow, sorry, Dad," she hissed, giggling with tension. "Not used to having you around again."

"Sure, munchkin, sure." He steadied his own breathing as he flattened himself against the wall and squinted down into the narrow strip of side garden.

There were shadowy figures running backward and forward. A body lay slumped against a low wall, black blood leaking from the lower abdomen. Someone noticed him on the second floor, and a rifle was pointed. Mac ducked back just in time, the bullet smashing through the window and burying itself in the ceiling with a snowy burst of plaster.

Sukie started to cry.

"Let 'em have it, Dad!" shouted Jack. "Go on, kill them."

Henderson McGill closed his eyes. The ragged figures outside were from a nightmare. He wasn't really standing there, holding an unfired shotgun, with four of his children behind him.

Of course he wasn't.

"Kill 'em, Daddy!" squeaked Sukie, giggling at her own nerve.

"Yeah," he said, nodding. "I'll do just that, sweetheart."

Pushing the barrel of the Brazzi through the shattered glass, he took hasty aim at the nearest of the daring silhouettes.

The gun kicked against his shoulder with a satisfying jolt. He peered out, disappointed to see that there was still only one corpse down in the trampled white of the garden.

"You get one, Daddy?" asked Jocelyn.

"Sure did," he said. "Plugged the critter plumb between his mean, ornery eyes."

DESPITE THE dead bolts and security devices, the raiders managed to break in the kitchen door. Jeanne and Angel kept them at bay for five or six minutes with steady fire from their handguns, but the mob outside had several sawed-down shotguns and used them to drive the defenders up off the first floor.

An overhanging porch ran the length of the back of the house, and Preacher Casey had encouraged his screaming followers to use it for cover from the defenders' shots.

Mac joined his wives, daughter and two sons on the first landing, opening fire on anyone stupid enough to show themselves.

John and Paul were both furious.

"Bastards will raid our food supplies once they get into the cellar," said the older boy. "Could finish us. Must be twenty still alive and unwounded."

"Can't have that." Mac glanced at them. "We stay up here and they steal everything. Might as well get killed quick as face that. Think of the little ones starving slowly to death."

"Should we risk attacking them?" asked Paul. "Lot of them."

"Sure. Rabble. Six of us, well armed. Six McGills against a raggedy mob. Let's go get the bastards! Check ammo."

"If we go down the stairs, they'll…" began John McGill.

"I'm going out on the roof. And you're coming with me. Shotgun each. Won't expect us attacking them through the broken kitchen door. Moment you hear us open fire, then Paul and Pamela come down to help. You two—" Mac pointed at Angel and Jeanne "—stay up here and guard the little ones. No matter what happens, you both stay put."

"I'd forgotten how forceful Mac could be," Jeanne said with a grin, kissing him lightly on the cheek. "Go get them."

IT WAS BITINGLY COLD and the shingles on the sloping roof were treacherous with ice. Mac and his son were both barefoot, picking their cautious way down. There was still bedlam from inside the first floor, with someone singing out an obscene parody of the good old hymn, "Shall We Gather at the River?"

There was deep snow piled at the eastern end of the porch, and Mac went first, gasping as he landed clumsily, twisting his ankle on rutted ice. But he was able to stand, wincing as he put weight on the right leg. John was quickly down at his side.

"You all right, Dad?"

"Sure. Can't run far, but I'm not figuring on doing any bastard running. Sure a squid like you can keep up?"

"At your shoulder, Dad."

McGill nodded, feeling a surge of pride and love for his boy.

He gripped the Brazzi tight, and John followed suit with the Winchester. He had a handful of shells in his pocket.

The door had been completely destroyed, the wood ripped apart by dozens of hacking ax blows.

"Need to layer it with steel next time," muttered John.

"Get the house back first."

His son clapped him on the shoulder.

Mac braced the shotgun at his hip, carefully stepping in over the splinters of painted wood, picking his way between the shards of broken glass.

A man and a woman were copulating on top of the table, taking it in turns to swig from a green bottle of wine. For several heartbeats neither of them took any notice as the two men appeared at their side.

Then the woman's mouth dropped open, showing toothless gums, and she drew in a long breath ready to scream.

Mac didn't hesitate. He pressed the muzzle of the Brazzi shotgun into the man's back, just to the right of his spine, and squeezed the trigger.

The sound of the shot was muffled, but the effect was utterly devastating. The shot tore through the liver, shredding it to rags, then carried on almost unchecked into the woman's lower stomach.

Mac knew enough about death to be certain he didn't have to waste another round on either of them.

The man rolled off, the back of his shirt flaring into yellow flames from the proximity of the blast. He was rigid with shock, arms spread as he crashed to the floor. Blood was pouring from the massive exit wound above the hip.

The woman lay on the table, legs splayed. Both hands had gone to the gaping wound in her belly, as though she was trying to stuff the yellowish coils of intestine back inside herself.

The man was making a harsh rattling sound in his throat, and the woman was gasping, her breathing fast and shallow.

Nobody else on the first floor of the house seemed aware that the avengers were among them.

Ahead of them, in the dining room, the light was on, and the singing was louder, accompanied by the smashing of glass. McGill had a moment to wish he'd put on his combat boots.

He glanced at John, whose face was white as death, eyes wide, mouth half-open.

"Here we go," he said, and the young man managed a nod of agreement.

It was a massacre.

Not one of the tatterdemalion gang even managed to fire a shot.

Mac stood to the left of the open door, John to the right.

The central figure in the room was standing at the head of the table, clutching a cognac bottle in his left hand, his right fondling the sagging breasts of a fat young woman.

The bottle was being used to conduct the singing of a revolting version of "Bringing in the Sheaves." He was skinny, aged around fifty, with a short-handled ax tucked into his belt. He was wearing a stained black denim shirt with a strip of white plastic pinned around his wattled throat like a deliberate parody of a clergyman's collar.

As soon as the two men opened fire, the room exploded in bedlam. Blood sprayed everywhere, walls and floor and ceiling dripping crimson. Bodies stumbled and fell. Men and women screamed and fought to get away from the ruthless execution. But the windows were barred, and the only exit from the room was blocked by the murderous shotguns.

It took less than ten seconds to butcher the majority of the raiders.

Both Mac and his son kept a single cartridge in the breech, standing ready.

The room stank of hot blood and shells and excrement, a smell that any soldier would recognize as the true scent of death.

Mac banged the butt of his Brazzi on the door. "Those who can walk, get the fuck out of my house. Take your wounded with you. All of them."

John slipped seven more rounds into his pump-action Winchester Defender. He fired one off above the heads of the dazed crowd to emphasize his father's words. "Move it!" he shouted, voice ragged and high with the tension.

From behind him, Mac heard Angel's voice calling out to him. "How is it?"

"Under control. The guests are just readying to leave."

He couldn't believe how he felt. His heart was going like a trip-hammer, his mouth was dry, and his hands were sweating. With the help of his son he'd just massacred at least eight or nine men and women. Slaughtered them at point-blank range. Gunned them down as they stood there helplessly.

And it felt so *good*.

One by one the survivors were getting to their feet, dragging up their wounded comrades. The screaming had stopped, and there was only a low moaning from the injured.

"I'll watch the back door," said John.

"Sure."

Mac noticed that his son's eyes were wide with shock. His face was dappled with smeared gobbets of crimson, his beard filled with tiny bright rubies.

Mac had snatched a moment to reload his own shotgun, covering the remnants of the murder gang as they slouched past him.

One short man muttered, "Didn't have to waste us all, mister. No harm."

There was a flaring temptation to take his head off with another shot. After so much death, one more wouldn't make any difference. But Mac managed to overcome the killing fever.

"Just get the fuck out," he said, calmly.

"Want help?" called his second wife.

"No. Stay there. Nearly done. Just the dead left to get rid of. We'll drag them out in a while. Deal with them later."

There were finally seven corpses, sprawled among their dining-room furniture. The ordinary chairs and table seemed to mock the grotesque stillness of bloody death.

Mac saw that one of the dead was the skinny man dressed like a priest, lying huddled up against the glass-fronted bookcase.

He stepped toward him, conscious of the hot stickiness between his bare toes. John called from the kitchen, making him turn away.

"All gone. Clear over the bottom wall and across Beulah Creek."

"Good. We'll..."

The corpse at his feet erupted into violent life, swinging at him with a vicious ax.

Mac parried the first blow with the barrel of the scattergun, the blade of the hatchet sparking off the blued steel.

"Messiah'll drink your fucking brains!" screeched the madman.

Mac jabbed at him with the gun, gripping the stock, unable to shift his hands to reach the trigger in case it gave the killer the chance to chop him.

"Dad?"

There wasn't even a splinter of a second to call out to his son; every particle of his mind was concentrating on the rheumy eyes of the lunatic in front of him.

"Yes, yes, yesyesyes..." The chanted words slithered into each other like a nest of tangling cottonmouths.

The scarred blade came in again, low, aiming for Mac's groin. But he was able to step back outside it, swinging the scattergun backhanded and catching the man a glancing blow on the side of the head.

Blood trickled from the long cut.

Mac was quick. He used the butt to knock the weapon aside, then dropped the Brazzi and got in close enough to use his hands.

Though he still wasn't back to the level of fitness he'd achieved before the *Aquila*'s last, doomed mission, Henderson McGill still remained an enormously powerful man.

His left hand gripped the mock-preacher's right biceps, fingers digging in like chromed-steel claws, separating the muscle from the bone and making Casey cry out in agony. The short-hafted ax cluttered into the puddled blood around their feet.

Mac's right hand had the helpless man by the throat, clamping off the air. Fingers crushed the windpipe, cracking the fragile thyroid bone, tighter and tighter, all of his vengeful rage flowing down his arms, into his hands.

The leader of the attackers was choking to death. His eyes protruded like the stops on a mission harmonium, his tongue flicking out like a rattler tasting the air, darkening, purpling. Blood was suffusing the man's face, and his hands clawed at Mac's arms, struggling desperately to loosen the death grip.

"Dad? You all right? Let go of him and I'll shoot the scum!"

"Waste of a good bullet," Mac said through clenched teeth. "No need, son."

With all his strength he hoisted the preacher off the floor. His feet drummed at Mac's shins, but there was no power left in them.

Crimson worms inched from the open mouth and from the corners of the eyes.

Breath croaked deep inside the man's throat, and he went limp. Mac didn't let go at first, still holding him in the air until he was sure that life was truly gone.

He dropped the corpse to the carpet to join the others.

"We'll clean up this mess in a while," he said, rubbing his hands on his pants. "First, though, I reckon we all deserve a mug of coffee."

5

For a few moments it seemed to Jim Hilton that the shooting had nothing to do with them or with the hovering Chinook.

The amplified voice carried on for several seconds, as though the speaker was oblivious to what was happening below them.

"We'll take you north, to the secret base. Code name is Aurora. Before we land there'll be identification and... What the sweet fuck is going on, Major?"

The noise was like someone tearing along a seam in a bolt of silk.

Kyle was closest to Jim, yelling. "What they shooting?"

"Don't know. Machine gun of some sort, I guess. Nanci?"

"Probably they've somehow managed to obtain a military SAW."

"What's that?"

"Squad Automatic Weapon. Replaced the good old M-60 years ago. Lighter and faster. Listen to it go. The M-265. Eight hundred rounds a minute. Put a hole in a steel helmet at a mile.''

The chopper had started to climb, slipping sideways toward them as it tried to dodge the stream of bullets from out in the desert. There wasn't just the machine gun, but the single shots of rifles, as well. The searchlight had gone off, but the loudspeaker was still switched on.

''Get the missiles primed, Major! Jesus, they hit us!''

Down on the ground they could hear the end, even before they saw the flash of fire. Lead sliced through the camouflaged fuselage of the big helicopter, perspex smashed, men yelled. The turbo-powered engine was faltering, then racing out of gear.

''That's it,'' Nanci shouted.

There was enough light now for them to see that the Chinook was doomed. One rotor had jammed, and the other was flailing erratically with broken blades. The whole body of the chopper was starting to revolve, nose up. Someone managed to get a missile off in those last, doomed seconds. It flew erratically into the air, straightening toward the west, and vanished, leaving only the pale, feathered plume of its vapor trail behind it.

The shooting had stopped abruptly, the hidden group of ambushers able to see that they'd achieved their aim.

"Look out!" shouted Jeff Thomas, throwing himself flat in the street, followed by Sly Romero, whimpering in terror.

But the rest of them could see that the tumbling helicopter wasn't going to come down all that near to them.

Like a demented banshee, the amplified voice gave a final truncated cry.

"Hilton... Aurora. North to... Oh, shi—"

There was a dazzling burst of light, blooming from near the tail of the Chinook. It was white-hot silver at its center, shading through gold to smoky crimson near its edges. There was surprisingly little noise for such a bright explosion, just a soft rumble that rolled out across the wilderness all around the old ghost town, echoing from the distant mountains in a whisper of sound.

The point of impact, as near as Jim Hilton could figure it, was around six hundred yards from the edge of Calico. Roughly northeast, in the general direction of the long-abandoned military installation of Fort Irwin.

The fire burned with a terrible crackling intensity for less than twenty seconds, then the night came flooding in again, riding on the back of an immense stillness.

"No point going to look for survivors from that," said Carrie.

Steve had helped his son to his feet, patting him on the shoulder to reduce the trembling terror to an occasional gulping sniff.

"That's the end." Jeff Thomas turned on his heel and started to walk quickly back toward their sleeping quarters.

Jim Hilton stopped him. "Wrong," he said. "Guess it's more like a beginning."

Kyle Lynch had brought out his Mannlicher .357 rifle and now he rested the stock gently on the stones by his bare feet. "You reckon those guys with the guns'll be coming in to see us, Captain?" he asked.

"Yeah." Nanci started to speak, but he talked over her. "They'll have heard the loudspeaker and know that we're here."

"Whoever they are," said Kyle.

"Could make a guess." Nanci Simms was looking around at the desolate ruins of the old township. "Best get ready for them, Jim," she said.

"Sure. But who do you think they are?"

She took him by the arm, leading him away from the others with a surprisingly strong grip. "You know that Jeff's told you I'm a teacher."

"Sure."

"Believe that?"

"No."

The older woman smiled at him. "Figured you didn't get to be doing the job you did by being a real idiot, Jim."

"My guess is something close to military Intelligence, Nanci."

"That's close enough for now. It's not right, mind, but it's close enough for now."

"So?"

"There's always plans, Jim."

"For what?"

Again came the smile, her teeth white in the moonlight. "For everything. President dropping dead in a bordello in Juarez. Chinese invading Alaska in sailboats. You name it and some government high-forehead little nerd will have produced a contingency plan for it. So, Earthblood wasn't entirely unexpected."

"Was it a plant cancer from one of our laboratories, Nanci?"

"Doesn't signify where it came from. It came, it bred and it conquered."

"Now its effect is passing."

She nodded. "Looks possible. Seen a few touches of green breaking through the dead red.

But it's done its stuff with great efficiency, and the world won't ever be the same.''

"Speaker shouted something, just before it went down, about a place called Aurora.'' He could smell the stench of aviation fuel from the crashed Chinook, over the ridge.

"Right. One of those contingency plans from Nerdsville.''

"North. You know where?'' Sudden hope flooded his heart.

"No. Sorry, Jim. I know a little about a lot, but things like Aurora were on a high need-to-know basis. Very high. Fifteen floors up over my poor old head.''

"The guys with the guns?''

"I heard about a kind of contra-grouping. Senior officers, some politicos, men with big money in industries. Powerful men. And a few women. Called themselves the Hunters of the Sun.''

Their conversation ended abruptly as the machine gun suddenly opened up again, bullets ripping through the weathered walls of what used to be the old schoolhouse in Calico.

THE CONTRAST with the time, only short weeks ago, when they'd been attacked back at Stevenson Base, was very considerable.

Then they'd all been severely disoriented, virtually weaponless and mentally unprepared to do much to defend themselves.

Time had passed.

Times had changed.

Now they were armed and more than ready to kick some ass.

Jim Hilton had taken charge of their defense, making sure that Sly and Heather were safely at their center. He picked a group of buildings near the top of a hill, overlooking the parking lot, placing everyone out in a skirmish line.

After that initial burst of firing, the attackers remained silent. The obvious guess was that they were closing in under cover of night. The moon had almost vanished behind a skirt of thickening cloud, and midnight was drawing nearer.

One major problem was that the defenders had no way of knowing how many men were out there. It could be only three or four. Then again, it could be half a regiment.

Jim gripped his Ruger Blackhawk Hunter, staring into the blackness, fingers firm on the cushioned grip with the walnut inserts. The thirty-five-ounce, six-shot, .44-caliber revolver felt right. Ready for use.

He'd put himself at the center. Nanci had gone to the far left, without being told, nearest to the last sound of shooting. She was dripping with weaponry: the scoped rifle on her shoulder, the matched Heckler & Koch automatics on the hips and the machine pistol in her hand.

Jeff Thomas had followed her, carrying his Smith & Wesson 4506, an eight-round .45. A broad-bladed butcher's knife swung on his left hip as he scampered after the tall woman.

Steve Romero was next, between the ex-journalist and Jim Hilton. The tall skinny radio expert had a polished bowie knife sheathed on the hip with a small blued Beholla .32 automatic balancing it. The unidentifiable sawed-off scattergun was in his right hand. None of his weapons would be much use above a range of twenty-five yards.

"But let the bastards get close," he'd said with a grin at Jim.

Kyle Lynch was next along from Jim Hilton, to the right, with the excellent Mannlicher rifle lying at his side. A Mondadori .32 automatic was holstered on his belt.

Carrie Princip completed their lineup. Like Steve Romero, she wasn't armed for distance. She had the Smith & Wesson 2050, the six-shot, .22 revolver with the snub, four-inch barrel.

Heather was resting flat on the ground, right behind her father. "Couldn't I have a gun, Dad?" she whispered to him.

"Sorry, kitten."

"Dad!"

"Sorry, honey. Forgot about calling you 'kitten.' Just stay there and keep quiet. If things go wrong, head out back and keep running."

"They aim to chill us, Dad?"

"You saw what they did to the chopper. Not too friendly."

The first noise was a single snapping round from Nanci Simms. The echo from the rifle rolled around them.

It was followed by a yelping gasp, and the clatter of someone falling down.

"One less, Jim," she called.

He thought he glimpsed someone moving out of the corner of his vision, but he couldn't be certain. The desert at night was eternally silent yet filled with an infinity of tiny sounds.

The voice seemed to come from about three hundred yards ahead of him. Immediately Jim checked behind to make sure it wasn't a trick to distract them. But there was nothing there.

"Yo, the camp! You hear us?"

"Don't say anything, Jim," hissed Nanci.

"I know that," he retorted, angry that she thought he could be that stupid.

"We don't mean no harm. Only that the chopper was after us. We haven't done anything to justify that kind of retaliation."

Whoever he was, the man out in the blackness was well educated, with a pleasant, convincing kind of a voice.

"Hello! Hello in there!"

The reply came from just to the left, behind Jim Hilton, making him jump.

"Hello!"

Steve Romero was quickest to react. "Sly. Keep your mouth shut."

"Man was friendly, Dad." The voice was soft, gentle and puzzled.

"Yeah, son. But he's not *really* a friend. Trying to trick us. Don't say a word. How do we keep our lips when we want to be quiet?"

"Huh?"

"When we keep quiet, our lips have to be...be what, Sly?"

A chuckle of delight. "Oh, yeah. Like a great big zipper."

"Good." Steve turned toward Jim. "Sorry 'bout that, Skipper."

"No problem."

"Nice one of you showed some manners. If he wants to come out here, then we'll guarantee his safety. Rest of you keep your silence, and we can't make any promises."

Jim kept checking behind him. There was just enough filtered moonlight for him to notice Nanci Simms doing the same.

"Losing patience. You saw what happened to the Chinook. Likely to find yourselves going down under a triple-red code." Anger flared in the voice. "We got the men and the firepower to wipe you out without a trace."

Sly spoke very quietly to himself. "Gee, Dad was sure right. Man isn't friendly. The painted smile's gone."

For over half an hour there was no more talk and no sign of life out in the raven black desert. Then the voice made one last effort. The anger had been carefully smoothed over, so that it was almost gone.

"Captain Hilton. Jim. We know who's there. Know about your mission. General Zelig's sent us to get you and Marcey Cortling and the rest of you and bring you to safety."

Marcey Cortling had been second in command of the *Aquila* and had been decapitated in the landing crash. It was odd that the invisible speaker knew so much and yet so little.

Out of cautious habit, Jim Hilton glanced behind him again, toward the township.

He saw half a dozen shadowy figures creeping toward him, less than twenty feet away.

6

Two months earlier Jim Hilton would certainly have hesitated for a fraction of a second, with his mind blurred by the sanctity of human life. Something to preserve, not destroy.

But that was then.

This was now.

The wide-spurred hammer clicked back, falling on the full-metal-jacket round.

The gun kicked, barrel seeking the sky. But Jim was braced and ready, wrist strong. Beyond the flash of the muzzle, he saw one of the figures go tumbling out of sight, as if someone had pulled a rug out under its feet.

There was no need to shout a warning to the others in his group. The boom of the GPF-555 Ruger was enough to alert them to the sneak attack.

Heather screamed and Sly jumped up, waving his arms as if he were being attacked by a swarm of vicious mosquitoes.

The clouds pulled away from the serene silver moon, enabling Jim to glimpse what they were up against. There were five or six men, three in dark-blue-and-black camouflage jackets. The others wore brown sweaters, with leather patches on elbows and shoulders. All were carrying Uzi machine pistols.

But the shock of Jim's lightning response had given the edge to the defenders of the ridge. Nanci had swung around like a scorpion, opening up with her own Port Royale machine pistol, spraying lead at the uniformed attackers.

Carrie's little .22 popped away at the end of the line, and Steve Romero's sawed-down shotgun roared, sending a jet of flame into the night.

Jim took careful aim and put down the farthest of the men, who'd already turned to try to run away. In the moonlight he saw a disk of smashed bone torn from the top of the skull, hurtling off into the night like a Frisbee, blood and brains erupting from the shattered head.

"Stop shooting!"

The voice belong to Nanci Simms, cutting through the savage exultation of the firefight. Jeff was last to check himself, another big .45 slug booming out across the sandy wasteland.

"We put them all down," she called, voice ragged, her tall figure loping toward Jim Hilton at the center of their defensive line.

"Sure?"

"Yeah. But there might still be some living. Come with me. Rest of you cover us. Jeff, you and Kyle watch out for any more coming in from the other side."

"They've still got that machine gun." Kyle was blowing hard, as though he'd just run five miles across sand dunes.

"Yeah," agreed Jeff. "They open up with that, and we're shredded meat."

"They just lost at least a third of their men. Maybe as much as two-thirds. They're hardly likely to rush us again, are they? See sense, Jefferson." Nanci turned to Jim. "Come on."

The pebbles rolled under his feet, and he had a sudden, irrational fear that he might fall and put his hand onto the face of a corpse. As they walked over the ridge and down the slope, Jim levered three more rounds into the big handgun.

"I counted seven," said Nanci. "Liked your shooting, Jim. Grace under pressure. You would be very surprised to know how rare that is. Ah, here's the first of the coolers."

The moonlight seemed to be getting brighter, and Jim found he was hunching his shoulders in anticipation of a sniper's bullet splintering his vertebrae into powdered bone.

The man was wearing one of the brown sweaters, patched at elbow and shoulder. His Uzi was a few feet away from him, muzzle down in a patch of soft, dark sand.

He'd been shot in the back, trying to run away, the bullet hitting him below the shoulder on the left side and exiting through the center of the chest, leaving a hole the size of a small plate.

"How d'you make sure they're really dead?" asked Jim. "I mean . . . not him. Obvious. But one of them might be faking it."

Nanci turned to him. "I confess that you choose the oddest moment for your queries. You don't bend over them and check the pulse beneath the ear, if that's your idea. That way you get your own throat opened up if they're 'faking it,' as you so appropriately put it."

Jim tried to ignore the sarcasm. "So how do you make sure?"

"Like this." She lifted her polished boot and stamped down, aiming the heel at the eye of the corpse. There was a horrible liquid grating sound. The head rocked, but the dead man didn't move.

"You do that and watch to see if they try to get up. If they don't, then it means they are no longer dwelling this side of the dark river, Jim."

All but one of their attackers had been killed outright or had died within a minute or so of being gunned down.

Some of them had several bullet wounds stitched across their chests or backs.

Nanci Simms kicked one of them over, pointing down with the muzzle of her machine pistol. "Haven't lost my touch," she said. "Look at that pattern. Trig and trim as an Amish quilt."

There were three 9 mm bullet holes in a straight line, perfectly spaced out.

Jim caught the faint rustle of a sound from a large clump of dead sagebrush to their right. The woman also heard it.

"Got him," she said very quietly.

Despite her height and age she moved with an uncanny balance and elegance, cat-footing her way toward the noise.

Jim Hilton started in to follow her, but she waved him back with a peremptory gesture of the Port Royale.

He stood in the stillness of the night, holding the Ruger loosely down at his side. Behind him the rest of their small group of survivors were waiting, and his mind began to tussle with the overwhelming problem of what they might do next. Where they might go.

But the adrenaline rush from the firefight was still flooding through him, and Jim found himself unable to look logically toward any sort of future. It was all too uncertain.

"Jim?"

"Yeah?"

"Here."

"He still alive?"

"Only just. Got his ticket for the last train west and one foot already aboard the caboose."

Mesquite crackled as he pushed through, finding the woman kneeling by a dark figure.

The man was on his back, moaning in a soft, bubbling voice. It was only just possible to make out an occasional mumbled word. Blood, black in the moonlight, was frothing around his lips, dappling the stark pallor of his face.

"Lungs," said Nanci. "And a couple of bullets through the guts." She laughed. "Think it was Carrie's popgun did the damage. Just shows that it's not the size but where you put it that really makes the difference."

"Any chance of finding out who he is? Who the rest of them are?"

"No. I'd work on him if I thought it was worth it. But his mind's locked away into his own passing. Too late."

Jim filed the casual, thrown-away reference to being ready to "work on him."

"Cold...feet frozen...can't any...didn't say guns ready..."

Nanci straightened. She swung her right foot back and kicked the dying man with surgical precision, the toe of her boot cracking into his head just below and behind the right ear.

The impact made a surprisingly quiet, moist thudding sound.

"That it?" asked Jim.

"Sure. That's it. I think we should go and rejoin the others now. Nothing more out here for any of us. He carried no identification at all."

"Think he was one of those . . . what did you call them, Nanci?"

"Hunters of the Sun? Very possible. I don't know enough about them to be certain of this sort of modus operandi. Trained men, well armed, clothed in a sort of uniform. Paramilitary grouping." She nodded, her pale blue eyes seeming almost white in the silvered light. "Would make sense. Think we were lucky, Jim. They didn't expect us to be well armed and ready for them. They won't be so careless next time.''

THE SOUND OF A TRUCK and several motorbikes came roaring out of the blackness roughly a half mile north of Calico.

Jim and Nanci Simms had only just rejoined the others, and they all stood, silent, listening.

"Going away," said Sly Romero, quickly recovered from the shock of what had gone down less than a half hour earlier.

"Right." His father nodded. "Good boy. They're going away, all right."

"How many dead?" asked Carrie.

"Seven. All of them that tried to sneak in and back-stab us. All dead." Realizing that he was still holding the heavy pistol, Jim slid it quickly into the oiled leather holster.

Heather was looking at him, and he took a hesitant step toward her, but the young girl turned away from him.

The sound of the engines was fading off to the north.

"Think they're really going, Nanci?" Jeff Thomas was shuffling from foot to foot, like a little boy bursting to go to the rest room.

"Yeah. And stop hopping around, will you. Look like you have to take a leak."

Carrie brushed dust off her hands. "If we keep a guard, we could maybe go back to bed."

"Sure," agreed Jim.

"Then what?" said Steve.

Jim didn't have any answer for that one.

7

The first yellow light of dawn came creeping in through the broken windows of the room where Jim Hilton and his daughter had spent the night.

The ceiling was stained and cracked plaster, decorated with a variety of graffiti. Some had been done with spray cans, but most of them showed the peculiar smeared effect of writing with a candle.

Heather stretched, the T-shirt tight across her shoulders. "Dad?"

"What is it, love?"

"I dreamed about Mom last night."

"I dreamed about her during the time I was coming home. And you and Andrea."

"It was just Mom and me."

He sat up, rubbing the stubble around the jawline. "Tell me, Heather."

She stood up, kicking her way out of the sleeping bag. "We were in a big art gallery. Like an old bus station, with lots of rooms. Metal galleries and walkways. Nobody else around. Pictures of saints and stuff. Lots of gold and reds and blues. Sort of nice.''

Jim rubbed sleep from his eyes, remembering that he'd helped to slaughter seven men only a few hours ago.

''Go on.''

''Mom was laughing at some of the pictures. Said that the infant Jesus had a fat ass in one of them. Made me laugh a lot.''

''Your mother was good at making people laugh,'' he said.

''Sure. Then I was looking at this picture that had some real triple-ape demons, with pincers and gallows. Looked up and she'd vanished, Dad. I was there all alone.''

He nodded. ''Then what?''

Heather shook her head, and he could see unshed tears glistening in her blue-gray eyes. ''That was it! Just that. I turned round, and Mom was gone. Just like she really went and . . .''

The girl's hand went to her mouth, and she scampered outside, bare feet padding in the soft California desert dust.

Jim followed her out, but respected her need for privacy. He moved toward Kyle Lynch and Steve Romero, who had got a fire going with the help of Sly. There was some instant soup bubbling away, its steam rising into the cool morning air.

Jim checked his wrist chron. "Coming up to seven," he said. "Good to have a quiet night. I thought I heard coyotes."

Jeff Thomas was carrying a pile of wood he'd collected around the backs of the surviving buildings in Calico. "Yeah. I heard them, too. Sounded like they were fighting."

Nanci Simms was walking just in front of him, looking like a fashion ad for outdoor casual wear for the older woman. The pants of her khaki pant-suit were tucked into the tops of the polished boots. She'd left the Port Royale behind, but the matched pair of automatics were elegantly holstered.

"They *were* fighting, Jefferson, dear. Fighting over the meat we so generously left out for their suppers last night."

"Supper?" said Carrie Princip, closing her eyes. "Oh, I get it. You don't think we should have maybe buried them? Not just allowed them to be torn by scavengers?"

Jim answered her. "No. Short and simple, Carrie. No."

Heather appeared, already dressed, her short blond hair brushed flat. She managed a small smile for her father as she squatted cross-legged on the ground by his side. Her eyes looked a little swollen.

Jim felt one of those inexplicable waves of overwhelming affection for his daughter and thanked the gods that he hadn't lost all of his loved ones. He reached out and took her small hand in his, getting a squeeze in return.

Kyle ladled out the soup into everyone's bowl, then helped himself.

There was silence in the circle as they spooned down their breakfast.

Jim was one of the first to finish, and he carefully took what seemed to be about one-eighth of what was left for his second helping.

"Decision time," he said.

Jeff jumped in first, wanting to know when they were going to get started on tracking down this mysterious Aurora place.

"Just head north, and we'll find it," he said, his right hand unconsciously stroking his badly broken nose. "Can't be that difficult."

"I was navigator on the old *Aquila*," said Kyle Lynch. "Means I know a little about maps. You should get that pea-size brain of yours into gear, Jeff, before you operate your mouth."

"What's that mean?"

"Means that 'north' isn't all that much of a peg to hang an expedition onto."

"If it's a sort of base, then it shouldn't be that difficult."

Kyle persisted, very gently. "How far north is north, Jeff?"

"Well, how the fuck should I know that? I don't know."

"Right. Fifty miles?"

"I said I don't know. But..."

"Hundred miles? Five hundred? Thousand miles north, Jeff?"

"Can't be that far! Where's a thousand miles going to put us?"

"Around about the Canadian border," said Jim. "That right, Kyle?"

"Yeah. Alaska is north, Jeff. That's another couple of thousand miles away from us. Be a good place for a secret base, after Earthblood, wouldn't it? Fancy trying Alaska."

"They didn't even say what 'north' really means, Jefferson, my dear boy." Nanci smiled at him as she spooned up the last of her soup.

"North means north. Come on, what the fuck else can it mean?"

"Hey, just tone the language down," warned Jim. "Got two young ones here."

Jeff's face was flushing with anger. His lips seemed to grow thicker and looser, and he'd begun to sweat. "Sure. Your precious little girl and that great dummy we got..."

Steve Romero was across and grabbing him by the neck before he could finish the sentence. "You want that nose broken again, Jeff?" he hissed.

"I didn't mean . . ."

Steve Romero was a good ten pounds lighter than the younger man, but he was about eight inches taller. He loomed over the journalist, face pressed close, his voice a threatening whisper.

"Sly isn't a dummy, you useless bastard! He's got Down's syndrome. Means he has some weaknesses. Also means that the boy's got some amazing strengths."

"All right, all right." Though Jeff Thomas's face was turning purple, nobody had stepped in to interfere.

Steve let him go and went and sat down, patting Sly reassuringly on the shoulder.

"You were talking about going north, Jeff," prompted Carrie.

Kyle interrupted. "Not likely they really meant absolutely hundred percent true north. North and west? North-northeast? We don't know. Chicago's north. Salt Lake City. New York. Vancouver. Bucksnort, Idaho."

Jeff was rubbing his throat. "Yeah, I get it. All right. You don't have to . . ." he mumbled, allowing the sentence to trail away.

Jim saw the look of hatred the ex-journalist darted at Steve Romero. And he wondered again what had really happened when Jed Herne had met his death in Jeff's company.

"Made your point, grease-ass." Jeff looked around at the others. "So, we don't know where we're going. So, what do we do?"

It seemed as if everyone started talking at once. Jim banged his spoon on the edge of his dish. "Hey, keep it down! One at a time, guys. Just one at a time, please."

Carrie raised a hand. He gave her a nod to carry on. "Thanks. Seems to me that we got a couple of choices. We can stay here, or someplace nearby, whatever suits us, and try and set up a commune."

"Like the peace-and-love hippies from last century." Jeff grinned. "Too much loving's far out of sight."

"That's really funny, Jeff," said Steve Romero. "I'm laughing so much it hurts."

Carrie ignored the interruptions. "Set up a community, if that's a better word. But we've all seen the sickness and madness that exists out there," she said, pointing vaguely toward the charnel house that had once been Los Angeles.

Nanci Simms cleared her throat as though she was about to speak, then she caught Jim's eye and changed her mind.

He stood up. "Carrie's right. That's one option. Try and find us our own little secure spot. But there's only eight of us. I doubt that'll be enough—" he hesitated as he looked for the word he wanted "—enough force, as things get tougher outside."

"You think we ought to try and find this place Aurora, Skipper?" Kyle Lynch shook his head. "I don't know. Means some blind traveling. Could be a hell of a lot more dangerous."

"Could be. But at least we know it's there. Zelig wants us, as well. Wanted us here. Sent us that doomed message in the chopper." Jim looked around. "We stay or we go? Which?"

8

Jim Hilton looked at the list he'd written in a notebook.

"Weapons are all right. I've written what everyone's got, including the ammo situation. We find any nine millimeter, it'd help a lot. But everyone's satisfied with what they've got. It would be good to find a small purse-size gun for Heather."

"How about Sly?"

"I'm not sure, Steve. You know better than we do about the lad. How would he get on with a blaster? Be able to cope?"

Steve rubbed his eyes. "I don't really know. I always wanted him to do what other boys did. It was very hard sometimes, but it mostly worked out. He knows he and Heather are the only ones without guns. But he said to me that she was a little girl. Sly sees himself as a man grown. Knows he's different. Knows he's not so clever. But he saved my life up in Colorado. Saved both me and Kyle."

Jim nodded. "Fine with me. It's your say-so in this, Steve. We manage to find us a couple of little

.32s around someplace, then they can have one each."

Nanci Simms was sitting cross-legged opposite Jim in the circle. All the adults were there, with Sly and Heather Hilton walking together up and down the main street, talking animatedly in the bright morning sunlight.

"Enough talk, Jim," said the older woman. "We've agreed to split up. Best chance that way. Cover some options. Then we can meet up again where we agreed. Muir Woods on December fifth."

A lot of the extended argument—running for more than two hours—had been about what the word "north" might reasonably mean.

Kyle had drawn up as accurate a map of the old United States as he could, laying in the lines of latitude and longitude.

Everyone agreed that the message about Aurora must mean it was more north than any other direction. So, assuming it wasn't as far away as Canada—or Alaska, as a better-natured Jeff Thomas pointed out—then it was possible to establish some sensible limited parameters.

Northern California was a strong candidate. Carrie mentioned the potential range of the Chinook sent by Zelig, with fuel capability being a factor.

"Way it went up...like swallowing an implode gren...makes it likely they were carrying some extra fuel aboard with them. Which means that speculations on the location of their home base are...are precisely that. Merely theoretical speculation."

Nanci's words torpedoed the Northern-California faction.

Oregon and Washington moved in as the joint favorites.

Jim clapped his hands together at that point, where everyone was getting very enthusiastic. "Look, it's going to be tough. Much tougher than most of us reckon. There's Northern Nevada," he went on, looking at Kyle's neat map. "Northern Utah. Definitely Idaho. Wyoming and Montana are also possibilities. Not such favorites, but we can't foreclose on where we go to look. The stakes are too great to make what could be a terminal mistake for all of us."

Nanci Simms nodded slowly. "Can't argue with any of that. I have serious doubts about Wyoming and Montana, but I don't deny the feasibility of either of them. Now, I have the best transport."

There was a ripple of laughter.

Kyle punched the air. "Kind of an understatement," he said.

The Mercedes would have looked good down on Rodeo Drive in Los Angeles. Out in the bloodied desert it was like a shimmering vision of the lost consumer society.

After the trauma of finding his wife dead and Heather's sister, Andrea, dying, Jim had made his way out toward Calico in a liberated Corvette that he knew one of his neighbors had put up on chocks in a rear garage. It had brought them within seven miles of their destination before the oil-warning light came on and the engine ground to a juddering and final halt on the hard shoulder.

He, Heather and Carrie had hiked the rest of the way, carrying all their camping gear and provisions on their backs.

Kyle, Steve and Sly hadn't arrived in the ghost town in much better shape.

The open-back pickup truck had started life about fifteen years ago as a Park Mescalero. But it had changed a lot in those years, acquiring bits of Fords and part of a Subaru and a chunk of a Volvo. They'd found it by sheer luck, not far from Kayenta, abandoned, with a half tank of fuel in it. The registration documents, tucked away behind the front seat, showed that it had been registered eleven months earlier, down in Chinle, in the name Hillerman.

The stripped, leathery corpses of two Navaho women had been lying alongside it. The scene of death had been a mystery with no explanation that made sense to Steve and Kyle. But they had managed to find some gas, and the truck had gotten them all the way down to Calico.

Now it squatted behind the tumbled remains of a store that had sold crystals. One tire was softer than soft, and the passenger door was tied on with baling wire. Much of the bodywork was a muted rust red color.

"You going cruising the valleys with the warm wind in your hair?" asked Steve Romero. "If you are, then you should dump that whining dwarf and take a real man along with you."

Jeff threw him the finger. "And fuck you, too, brother," he said.

"We split up." Jim got that in, recognizing that was where things were moving. He wanted to make it appear as if it was his idea, since he was the theoretical leader of the group.

"How?" Jeff looked around. "Don't think you're going to get your hands on the Mercedes, just because you were captain of a crashed spaceship, Hilton. You hear me?"

Jim stood up, hand on the butt of the Ruger. "If I wanted to take the car, Thomas, then I'd take it. You wouldn't stop me." Catching Nanci's cool blue gaze, he added, "Nobody would." He hoped to God that she didn't choose to challenge him.

She didn't, merely smiling gently at him. "But don't you think it might be better if I took it? I'm used to it, and it only seats two. May be better if I carry on with Jefferson here. I'll take the easterly route, sort of scurry around, and then we can make that December fifth deadline."

He nodded. "I'll stick with Kyle, Steve, Carrie and the two kids in the pickup. We'll try and go more directly north. How's that sound?" He looked around the small group for reactions.

"Yeah," said Jeff Thomas, who was watching Nanci Simms fixedly with the odd fascination of a rabbit in front of a cobra.

Steve Romero grinned. "Why not? I'll go tell Sly we're moving."

"We'll get away within the hour," Jim said. "Make the most of the daylight. Tell Heather, as well, will you, Steve?"

"Sure."

"Carrie?"

"I don't know about this, Jim. Aren't we stronger together?"

"In some ways. But we've got so much ground to cover."

Kyle Lynch was juggling with four small rounded pebbles. He let them fall and brushed his hands clean. "I agree, Jim. But I wish one of us had thought to pick up some decent radios. Transceivers. Talk and listen. That way we could all keep in touch, even over a good distance."

"Got a couple in the trunk," said the older woman casually. "Maybe Steve ought to come look at them. We can agree on frequencies."

She got up and walked slowly toward the parked sports car, Jeff tagging along on her heels like a little puppy.

Kyle Lynch whistled tunelessly between his teeth. "Not healthy the way he trails around after her. Nanci's old enough to be his mother. Strike that. Make it grandmother. I know he has it coming, but he's looking to get hurt."

Carrie laughed cynically. "Ever occur to you, Kyle, that getting hurt might be just what Jeff wants? Think about it."

"I don't get it, Carrie."

"I do," said Jim Hilton. "I've seen them a couple of times when they didn't know anyone was watching. Kind of sick."

The tall black navigator leaned forward. "Come on, I'm fascinated."

Carrie shook her head. "What they used to call playing Sadie-Maisie, Kyle."

"How's that?"

"Domination. That's the name of the game. Him slave, her mistress."

"Oh, you mean like... Surprises me that an arrogant bastard like Jeff would be subservient to anyone. 'Specially an old woman like Nanci. Though she's in... Oh, forget it. I really don't think I want to think about this."

They moved off to gather up their belongings and check out their vehicle. It didn't take them long to get ready to leave the ghost town.

"How about Mac?" asked Carrie Princip. "Only a day past the fifteenth, Jim."

"I know it."

"Anything could've happened to him and Pete Turner to delay them a little."

"Yes, I thought about that. I'm going to leave them a message."

"Where?"

"I've written a short report, detailing what happened. It'll also be useful in case Zelig sends anyone else down here after us."

"Where are you going to hide it?"

"Where would you put it, Carrie? You know Henderson McGill."

"Not as well as you, Jim. Still... I guess I'd put it in the saloon." She was grinning broadly as she saw from his expression that she'd guessed right.

"Yeah. Behind the bar, under a pint glass. Tell him about Muir Woods on the fifth. Maybe he'll find it. Maybe."

9

Jeff Thomas sang along with the tape that Nanci had slipped into the car's sophisticated player. It was a collection of the best girlie rock groups of the past five years and included some of his special favorites.

She'd stolen it for him in an unusually tender moment while they were living up in his Jackson Street apartment.

The thought of San Francisco reminded him of Nanci's warning to Hilton while they'd been finalizing routes.

She'd told him that the beautiful city on the bay was now a death trap where shadows clung to your shoulder and the juvenile wolf packs hunted along the urban canyons.

"An abundance of rotted corpses, Jim," she'd said in that old-fashioned, pompous way she had. There were times that he wanted to creep up behind Nanci and smash something heavy into that neat head. Pulp the bones and mash the brains and curdled blood.

But fear stopped him, fear that he might not make it without her. Fear of losing the most wonderfully exciting relationship he'd ever had in his life, the sickening thrill of ritual humiliation at her hands.

As soon as they'd left Calico, turning onto the wide, deserted swell of Interstate 15, Nanci had made him unzip his jeans so that she could fondle him as she drove, occasionally making him whimper as she dug her nails into him.

After a quarter hour she'd become bored and made him zip himself up again, ignoring his whimpered request for some kind of relief.

"Later, Jefferson," she'd said not unkindly. "When you've earned it."

But that was forgotten. The late afternoon was beautiful, and the engine purred along. They passed an occasional wrecked car, rusting away, sometimes with a jumble of whitened bones close by.

They didn't see another living soul.

The wind raced through Jeff's long hair, and he leaned his right arm over the sleek side of the Mercedes, feeling the welcome coolness.

The tape rolled on.

The night's getting light,
And the day's got so dark,

We're never goin' t' stop
To find some place to park.
Heading for tomorrow,
'Cause the dead have got today.
We're running close to empty
With the price we got to pay.
Yeah, the price we gotta pay.

His fists were drumming on the dash, and he was yelling out the lyrics as they drove on north and east, toward the Nevada state line.

THERE WAS a croaking, grinding noise from the overheated engine, and a spurt of noxious brown smoke from the exhaust.

"Again," called Kyle.

Steve was in the cab, head out of the window. "Trying to get this mother into gear's like stirring a basin of cold grits."

The pickup had sounded brash and confident as they gunned their way down the sandy main street of Calico, following the glittering chimera that was Nanci and Jeff in the silver Mercedes.

Kyle had been driving, with Sly next to him and Steve completing the front-seat lineup. Heather had been huddled on the sleeping bags, the hood of her sweatshirt pulled over her head to try to protect her from the billowing clouds of orange dust. Jim had his arm around her, fighting to compensate for the bucking of the rig over the rutted trail. Carrie was hanging on in the rear corner, braced against the rolling and rocking.

They'd barely reached the freeway when the truck started to play up. It began to cough and miss, making their motion even more jerky.

"Malfunction, Captain!" shouted Carrie, trying to lighten the moment.

But they were only a mile and a half toward Barstow when the pickup came to a silent, gentle halt. Everyone got out, their feet scuffing on the sun-baked, oily pavement.

They'd tried to analyze the fault and get her going again. Nearly two hours later they were still there, still trying.

"Cleaned the plugs," said Kyle. "It's not that."

"And we put in more oil," Jim added. "Not the hoses, either."

"Should send for the doctor." Sly had made the joke within a minute or so of the breakdown and had been rewarded with a round of laughter. Encouraged, he'd been making the same joke every quarter of an hour, downcast that nobody seemed to think it was funny anymore.

Jim walked to the center of the freeway, standing there and staring blankly out across the sunlit, shadowed landscape. A large bird was circling far above his head, way too high for him to identify it.

Apart from that, there was nothing moving. Heat haze shimmered over the desert.

Kyle, Carrie and Steve drifted across to join him, none of them wanting to break the silence.

Finally it was Carrie who spoke. "Now what do we do?"

Steve Romero scratched his neck where an insect bite flared crimson. Behind them his son was sitting in the minimal shade at the side of the broken-down truck. Heather Hilton was flicking stones, underarm, at a sign that told them that Barstow was four miles west.

"Maybe there's a mechanic in town," Jim said.

Kyle flicked sweat from his forehead. "That's a long shot. How come none of us know enough about the internal-combustion engine to figure out what's wrong here? Astronavigation and quantum physics we can do with our eyes shut. Truth is, we're not ready for this new world."

Carrie laughed. "We're the intellectual elite of our generation, gentlemen. But any redneck with the intelligence quotient of a fence post would be doing better than us."

"I'll phone in to the AAA," said Jim. "No. No, that's pointless. Think that my membership's lapsed a good while back."

"Seriously, Skipper," said Steve.

"Yeah, it's serious. Of course it is. Never mind the plans about Aurora and Muir Woods in three weeks' time. We need to worry about hiking in to Barstow. It'll take us a good two hours, with what we'll need to carry with us. And I don't figure they'll greet us with open arms."

"You came in that way to Calico."

"Right, Kyle. But by then we were on foot and we circled around any towns. Kept seeing the word 'outlanders' for strangers and signs that sort of whispered that we wouldn't live too long if we tried to pay a courtesy call on the good folks."

There was a sudden loud crackling from behind them. Heather had gotten bored and taken out the radio that Nanci had given them.

Sly clapped his hands. "Use the wonky-tonky!" he shouted excitedly.

"Don't play with that," called Jim. "It's not a toy."

"Can't I try and pick up someone on it, Dad? I know how to use one of these."

"All right, but be careful with it."

Steve Romero laughed. "Got more chance of snow in Death Valley, Heather. I've swept all the wavelengths, and there's plenty of nothing."

The girl turned the main control dial, producing different levels of background static. Then came a fragment of a human voice, and then more static.

"Go back!" shouted Jim, running over to his daughter and reaching for the set. "Back a little way on that control. Gently."

"Chill out, Dad. I've got it. I think...just about here..."

"Hallelujah, brothers! I'm here to bring repentance to the sinner and salvation to the faint of heart and pure of spirit."

Steve punched his right fist hard into his left hand. "I know that voice."

"Who?" said Carrie. "Not the same guy we heard when we were coming down in the *Aquila?*"

"Yeah. Jeremiah was his handle."

The voice was loud and clear, booming out of the little plastic Kayawa set. Heather winced and turned down the volume.

"I'm speaking here from the mental village under a murderous sky. I'm sometimes known as the daring sleeper, but others, praise their names, call me the imp of the perverse. You may call me 'René', if there's anyone out there listening to the bard from Barstow. Over and over and *O...U...T* spelling 'Out.' Y'all come see Jeremiah, voice in the wilderness and friend to the coyote. Come in."

"Give it me, Heather." Jim held out his hand for the radio.

"No. I can do it."

In a moment of irrational anger, he nearly slapped his daughter, then he controlled himself. "Give it to me. Now," he said.

The girl recognized the hard, cold edge in her father's voice and handed him the set, turning on her heel, mouth set in a sullen pout.

"Come in, Jeremiah. This is Jim Hilton of the *Aquila*. Over."

There was a long delay.

The small radio hissed and cheeped. Jim noticed that the hunting bird had zeroed in on some invisible prey. Hurtling, wings folded, it pulled up bare inches from the desert floor, seeming to have just missed its target.

He pressed the Send button and tried the call again.

"Hello, Jeremiah. Spoke a few weeks ago as we came in on the *Aquila*. You told us first about Earthblood. Remember? Over."

"Remember you well, Jim. Heard that your ship came in fast and hard. Glad you managed to make it through. Loud and clear this time. You must be somewhere round the Mohave to be scaling nineteen from twenty for volume. Over."

On an impulse, Jim Hilton decided that he wouldn't immediately give away his location to this crazed prophet of the airwaves.

"Not far, Jeremiah. Not far. You in Barstow? How are things there? Strangers welcome? Over."

"Welcome as broken glass in your breakfast cereal. Fresh as tomorrow's sunrise. Hallelujah, Brother Jim! Many in your party?"

"Half a dozen. Over."

"That's a fine, strong fifty per cent of the Savior's blessed sacred apostles, Jim. Sure you haven't got one called Judas Iscariot hidden in among your number? Over."

For a fleeting instant, Jim had a vision of Jeff Thomas, but he dismissed it from his mind.

"What we have is a broken pickup, Jeremiah. Know anybody around Barstow might come lend us a hand? Over."

"Give us your fix, brother."

"Coupla miles west of Calico ghost town. North side of the interstate. Over."

"Heard there was some shooting last night over your way. Over."

"Right. Helicopter came in from the north, and some guys opened up on it from the desert outside Calico. Blew it up. Over."

"What happened to them?"

"Chopper or the others? Over."

"Others. Saw the flash of the Chinook going right on down. *Requiescat in pace.*"

"Some of the others got hurt. Rest vanished."

There was a long pause. Everyone had gathered around the black-and-silver radio, listening intently to the static.

"That the doctor man?" asked Sly.

"Could be," replied Steve. "Wait and see, son."

"You there, Jeremiah? Over." Jim Hilton waited.

"Sure. Two miles west of Calico. Puts you around five miles from me. Be there in a half hour. Look out for me. Don't take any wooden nickels, Jim. This is Jeremiah from Barstow saying over, out and Hallelujah!"

10

"What are we looking for, Nanci?"

The older woman seemed to have an uncanny knack for finding good campsites. Though she'd told Jeff that she hadn't been in that part of the country for twenty years or more, she still seemed to know every side turning and where it would take them.

Early on Nanci had said that they were going to detour around Las Vegas. "Used to know a man there, a man called Flagg. Had some power. Might be dead now, might not."

They'd cut off through a nonexistent blip on the map, called Icebucket Wells, then along the flank of the Spring Mountains, passing close to an Air Force base, but the road southward to it was blocked by a huge tangle of burned and rusted metal. Nanci stopped the car, letting the engine idle while she stared stone-faced at the wreckage.

"Gas tanker ran into a couple of M-754s. Big tanks. And there's the remains of some APCs, as well. The way I read it, the base was being defended in numbers. Somebody took exception to that and came in fast and heavy."

She slowly turned the wheel, easing the powerful sports car toward the north. They advanced across Sarcobatus Flat, then made a right at Tonopah, where someone fired a ranging shot at them from behind the ruins of a gas station.

Nanci took no notice, hanging a left up 376, into Big Smokey Valley.

Which was where they stopped for the night, pulling off into what had once been a picnic area on the right of the narrow road. Nanci edged the vehicle past an abandoned camper truck and stopped finally near a fast-flowing stream, among the dead stumps of a grove of Sitka spruce.

It drizzled as evening came crawling in from the east, lurking behind banks of high cloud. Nanci put up the soft-top, bringing in the heater with a gentle warmth.

As the afternoon had slipped by, Jeff had dozed, enjoying the comfort and the security. Now, in the security and darkness, with a thin layer of snow on the higher ground around them, he felt as close to happiness as he'd felt for longer than he could remember.

Nanci touched him on the arm as they sat for a moment in the peace and stillness.

"At one with the wonders of nature, Jefferson?" she said quietly.

"Yeah. Reminds me of that old, old vid. My father had a worn copy. Three guys on motorbikes, hogging across the place. They all get wasted. One says something about how this . . ."

"Used to be a hell of a good country once," she concluded, giving him a rare smile. "I know it, too, Jefferson."

"I like being with you, Nanci," he whispered, amazed and scared by his own daring.

"That right?"

"Yeah. What is it we're looking for? You got an idea, don't you?"

She pursed her mouth, and he almost winced, anticipating some kind of violence. But she smiled again. "Aurora? North? Sounds like the land of Oz. We're following the yellow brick road. I don't have the ruby slippers, but I got me some shining black leather boots, don't I?" He didn't answer immediately and she touched him on the hand. "Do I not, Jefferson, with very thin, spiky heels?"

"Sure do, Nanci."

"I don't know what you are, sonny boy. Cowardly lion? Straw man? Tin man? Bit of the cowardly lion. Bit of the wicked witch, as well. If you were holding a whip, Jeff, then you'd love to use it.

Someone else has the whip, and you're on your belly, kissing it, aren't you?''

He didn't say anything, but this time she didn't seem to mind.

A flurry of snow blew against the car, making it rock slightly.

Nanci stretched and yawned. "Enough of this," she said. "Tent and fire, Jefferson. Something to eat, then..." She laid the palm of her hand flat across his crotch, laughing quietly at his instant response. "Jump to attention, don't you? Well, some food first, then we'll see about other needs maybe."

JEFF THOMAS HAD LIVED most of his life in and around cities. It didn't mean that he hadn't experienced some rough times early in his career when he was a fire-eating and profoundly ambitious young reporter, seeking out all the danger spots that the ailing planet could offer.

The first of his brace of Pulitzers had come after he'd spent eight months locked into a state mental hospital, under total cover, investigating allegations of physical and mental abuse.

There had been three suicides among staff the first week his articles ran in the *West American*.

His second major award had come when he successfully infiltrated a cadre of high-ranking spies in London. That had led to a grotesquely bungled attempt on his life, which he'd later inflated to more than it had been.

But Nanci wasn't quite right about Jeff, and not quite wrong.

He wasn't exactly a coward.

If risking his life might advance his career, he'd do it. And, like a cornered rat, if his life was threatened, Jeff Thomas was capable of rapid and violent action.

Even capable of a sort of courage.

MUCH LATER that night, huddled in the double sleeping bag, trying to steady his breathing, he touched Nanci with a hesitant hand.

"What is it, lover man?" She rolled over, and he could taste her breath on his face.

"Just... that I'm happy to be with you."

"Sure you are," she said. "Sleep well, Jefferson."

Angered and hurt at the cool rejection of his tentative whisper of real affection, he felt his eyes prickling.

"SOMETHING'S COMING," said Sly Romero, his narrowed eyes searching westward.

"You sure?" asked Jim Hilton. "I don't see anything, son."

"Me hear it, Captain Jim."

"Then I'm sure you're right." He half closed his own eyes, head on one side, straining to catch what it was the teenager had heard.

"Yeah," said Carrie, joining them. "Look, there's the dust."

Back before Earthblood, the freeways were always kept swept and clean. Now they'd all seen banks of mud or dirt piled high at the shoulders. Jim spotted the tiny trail of gray, almost invisible against the background of the desert.

"Could be Jeremiah, could be someone else. Better be careful. Steve, see if you can pick him up on the radio."

"Sure."

"Wonky-tonky," shouted Sly excitedly. "Over and in and over and out."

The dark speck was coming closer, approaching them at a surprisingly sedate speed that to Jim's practiced eye looked close to fifty-five miles per hour.

"This is Steve Romero calling Jeremiah. Calling Jeremiah. Over."

There was the usual roaring hiss of static, then came the familiar voice. "Well, here's a big scale-ten hallelujah for you folks. Now's the time of dogs burning and locusts whelping in the capitals of the world. Open the seventh seal, Brother Steve, and we'll get the altered altars into the knave's naves. Be with you in around two minutes and forty-five seconds. Hallelujah and out, from the one, the only, wilderness prophet.''

Steve pushed his thumb onto the Off button. But just before the set clicked into silence, they all clearly heard another voice.

''Ordinates on map refer—''

''Put it on again,'' said Jim. The first beat of his heart thrilled to the thought that this could well be Zelig. The second beat chilled at the acute realization that it could also be the men of darkness. What had Nanci Simms called them? ''The Hunters of the Sun,'' he whispered to himself.

But this time there was only an endless burst of crackling.

''Who?'' said Kyle.

''No idea. But whoever it was, they've just hit on the same wavelength that Jeremiah's been using. Sooner we get moving from here the better.'' Jim looked back at the lowering sun. The speck was now less than a mile away.

The six companions stood grouped together, the adults all holding their guns.

''What kind of rescue wagon's that?'' Heather asked as the vehicle drew to a smooth stop about fifty yards down the highway.

Colored fluorescent pink, it was a small glass-sided van with a huge yellow fiberglass ice-cream cone on top, next to a fifteen-foot whip aerial. On the side were painted the words: Tinklabell For The Terrific Taste!

The man who stepped out of the vehicle looked to be around fifty, of average height and build. He had on horn-rimmed spectacles and he was wearing a neat gray-brown three-piece business suit and dark maroon tie. His brown shoes were highly polished.

"This is Jeremiah?" exclaimed Kyle Lynch. "The guy looks like he's just come by to sell us life insurance."

"Good afternoon," said the man in a quiet voice with a faint Florida hint to it. "My name is Joseph J. Sirak, Jr." Seeing their bewilderment, he laughed. "Apologies, ladies and gentlemen. Of course. The *J* stands for Jeremiah."

"Hallelujah," breathed Jim Hilton.

11

Joe Sirak—it didn't seem possible to think of this gentle and respectable-looking man as the foaming prophet, Jeremiah—carefully rolled up his sleeves and placed his jacket on a black plastic hanger with the words Harknett Family Hotel on it.

"Now, let's see precisely what your problem is here."

He went to his ice-cream van and rummaged in the back, emerging with a handful of polished tools while everyone watched him in stunned, respectful silence.

Then he went to work on the pickup, accompanied by his whistling and the noise of chinking metal from under the hood.

"Could someone give it a try, please?"

"Sure." Steve hopped into the driver's seat and turned the key.

There was a moment of hesitation, then the engine coughed into life. Smoke poured for a few seconds from the exhaust, then swiftly cleared.

"Terrific, Joe," said Jim. "What was wrong with it?"

Sirak emerged from behind the pickup, wiping his hands on a spotless hank of cotton rag. There was a broad smile on his face. "Guess you could say that it was a little of everything, Jim." He put on his jacket again and adjusted his tie, which had slipped a quarter inch.

"Brilliant," said Carrie. "Saved our lives, Mr. Sirak."

"Call me Joe. Or Jeremiah. I'll answer to either of them. Saved your life, did you say?"

"Sure did."

He nodded, the smile vanishing as though someone had thrown a switch.

"Is that a figure of speech, young lady? Or do you realize that there is many a true word spoken in jest?" There was the briefest hint of the prophet Jeremiah in his words now.

"You mean that you think there's real danger, Joe?" asked Jim Hilton, looking instinctively all around them. But nothing was moving in the wasteland of eastern California.

"Mankind is always in danger. We give birth astride a grave, don't we, Captain Hilton?"

"Danger from what? From who? From where, Joe? You got the ears with your radio. Tell us what you've been hearing."

Sirak ran a comb through his black hair. "I've heard too much. As soon as Earthblood became a matter of public domain, the airwaves began to hum. Then, when the deaths started, you couldn't turn the dial without picking up a thousand calls for help. Aid the afflicted, they say. What could anyone do?" He stopped and dabbed at his eyes with an immaculate linen handkerchief. "The voices stopped quite quickly."

"We picked you up when we were coming down." Steve shook his head. "Christ, it seems to be only a couple of days ago. The very first time we heard about Earthblood."

Joe sighed. "Now you can go from zero up to infinity and you hardly hear a squeak. Just now and again, you know."

"You know anything of General Zelig, Joe?" Jim thought a moment. "Or Aurora? Or some outfit called the Hunters of the Sun?"

Joe glanced at his wristwatch. "I believe it's time that I was returning home again to Barstow. You must look me up—5498 Cuchillo Boulevard. There's a six-o'clock curfew in operation, and the men on the barrier enjoy their little, little power."

"Didn't hear the answer to my questions, Joe. That mean the answer was yes to all of them?"

"Affirmative."

"Tell us."

Sirak was beginning to perspire. "Don't press me, please, Jim."

"One at a time. Zelig?"

"Mentioned that name in the days when society was finally cracking up. Heard it since. That chopper that was shot down..."

"Yeah?" Jim touched the man on the arm. "Look, nothing'll happen to you. I'm like a guy playing blindfold chess on a board with no pieces. If you can help us..."

"Never saw myself as being in the same section of the field as the Good Samaritan," said Sirak, managing a worried smile.

"Aurora?"

"Some kind of center where a lot of military and some senators and folks have got together. Secret base is what it sounds like to me. Hear the name of Zelig linked to it."

"Where?" asked Kyle.

"North is all I know."

"Can you locate it more closely than just north?" asked Steve Romero.

"The car doctor's done good, hasn't he, Dad?" said Sly suddenly and loudly.

Joe Sirak smiled at the boy. "Neighbors of mine, years ago, had a lad like him. Such a sweet... No, I can't place it for you. Though..."

"What?" said Jim, picking up on Joe Sirak's hesitation.

"I wouldn't wish to place my life savings on this, but I get the feeling from direction and strength of some of the signals, that it could be Washington State or Northern California, or just across the border into Canada." He shook his head, fingers fumbling at the mother-of-pearl buttons on his vest. "Life savings! Listen to me. What's a dollar worth nowadays? Can't even wipe your backside on it. Light a fire with it. Life savings. Huh!"

"The Hunters?"

"Never heard that name. Not exactly. But Mr. Zelig . . . I mean *General* Zelig, and his men aren't the only sort of organized group. There are others. Cold and efficient. Never give time for a fix on them. Broadcast from every which place."

Jim began to feel uneasy.

Once when he'd been up on vacation with Lori and the girls, who'd have been only seven or eight at the time, they'd stayed at Many Glaciers Hotel in the national park.

He'd wanted to go backpacking for a couple of days, so he'd hiked off on his own. Lori and the twins had been perfectly happy to stay at the beautiful resort hotel, sunbathing and boating on Swiftcurrent Lake.

On the first evening he'd been readying himself for camping. Jim hadn't seen a single soul for the past five hours and was just beginning to find the majestic stillness of the woods oppressive, followed by a profoundly uneasy feeling.

As if he was being watched from somewhere. He knew what to do if he came across a grizzly, and the bell on his pack had been jingling merrily.

He took care to put anything edible in a pack and haul it high off the ground. Even as he'd lain down in the survivalist sleeping bag, Jim had made sure that his Ruger Blackhawk was in there with him.

Oddly he'd slept soundly and dreamlessly, waking in the refreshing cool of a Montana dawn, to find the deep paw marks of a very big grizzly all around him in the damp earth.

That unease was swelling within him now, making the hairs on the nape of his neck start to bristle and his lips grow dry.

"We'd better go," he said abruptly.

"I think that's best, too," agreed Joseph J. Sirak, Jr.

"Come along with us. We could use a man with your mechanical skills," suggested Kyle.

"I'm afraid that's not possible. I have commitments to my family." He touched his chest lightly. "And the old pump isn't quite as reliable as it once was." Shaking his head, he said regretfully, "No, I fear I have to decline. But I wish you all the best of luck."

"Thanks. We'll try to keep in touch with you on the radio."

"Steve, I hope you can. And if I should hear anything that might benefit you all, I'll do what I can to pass it along to you."

Everyone shook hands with the smartly dressed man, watching him as he climbed back into his unlikely vehicle.

"Listen to this," he called, beaming with delight from the driver's window.

A silver trombone came creakily out of the heart of the huge ice-cream cone, while a hidden speaker blew a tinny fanfare. And a trilling chorus opened up with: "Tinklabell, Tinklabell, the best for you and me, Tinklabell, Tinklabell, for all the famileeeee."

Sly clapped his hands. "Can me have a triple Rocky Road, please Dad?"

"It's not a real ice-cream van, son. Sorry. Not many places selling that sort of stuff nowadays, I'm afraid."

Joe Sirak waved a friendly hand and set off toward Barstow, moving, as before, at a very steady fifty-five miles per hour, never to be seen by any of them again.

Thanks to his help with the pickup, they were able to get well on their way without further incident, looping around Joe Sirak's hometown and heading on toward Bakersfield.

Night was falling and the weather was deteriorating when they came around a bend in the highway, straight into the roadblock.

12

The stone was simple, carved by Henderson Mc-Gill himself, using one of the old paving slabs that had lined their backyard in Mystic.

The lettering wasn't that regular, and the spacing was shaky, but the message was all too clear and readable.

Helen McGill. February 14, 2031–November 19, 2040. Beloved daughter of Angel and Henderson. We miss her so much.

It had been pneumonia.

They had a good stock of assorted drugs, but the young girl had failed to respond to any of them. One of the antibiotics that they tried had produced a violently reactive side effect. Helen's lips and tongue became swollen, and the inside of her mouth had peeled so that shreds of skin hung like yellowed lace.

The fever consumed her, though they'd swaddled her in blankets doused with snow. Helen had lapsed into unconsciousness on the third day of her illness and slipped away from them at two in the morning on the fourth day.

Angel took it hardest. "We've come through so much," she said after the dismal funeral, dry-eyed, tight lipped. "So much and we still managed to stay together."

"There wasn't anything we could've done." Mac held her hand while all of the family sat around the shadowy living room.

"No. I know that. But our little girl's gone. My first-born child, Mac. Sounds Biblical, doesn't it? Taken by the plague. Those cold-hearted scientists—no conscience, just damn stupid arrogance. Sitting around in their clean white coats and their sterilized laboratories. Playing their clever, clever games in glass tubes and microscopes. What they did killed Helen. Not the pneumonia. Two years ago we'd have taken her to the hospital, and they'd have saved her."

Then in silence they waited for the misery to fade, but acceptance and the lifting of the dreadful sense of loss would be a long time coming.

The weather changed, too, immediately after the burial, becoming unseasonably warm with ice and snow dripping off the dead, overhanging boughs of the trees in Howell's Coppice. Somehow their pain, tamped down by the demands of survival, would have been easier to bear in the cold grip of acute winter.

A moist southerly blew across New England, bringing the noon temperature up to fifteen degrees above freezing.

It made everyone moody and mean. Brother snapped at brother and wife at wife. Mac took Paul and John out hunting with him, going into the scrubland to the north of Mystic.

They came back with a deer, killed by the older boy with a single clean shot to the head.

It had been a successful expedition, apart from one unsettling factor.

John had been leading the way, rifle cradled under his arm, pushing through the muddy slush. Mac and Paul were following close behind him, carrying the deer between them.

They had been less than a half mile from home when someone had called out to them. A hoarse man's voice, strained and high, as though the speaker was trying to conceal his identity from them.

"You jes' best look out for us. We know all 'bout you and we'll get you! You won't fucking know where or when."

John had brought the gun to his shoulder, but Mac warned him not to shoot.

"Waste of a good bullet. Just some crazy out there, feels like letting go."

"Yeah, but there was that broken window last week," Paul had said.

"And someone crapped in the front path a couple days ago." John had spat angrily in the dirt at his feet.

The shout wasn't repeated, though they'd heard crashing in the undergrowth as if someone was running hurriedly and clumsily away.

There were no more such incidents after that, and when they finally got back to Melville Street, coming in the back way, over Beulah Creek, it was closing in toward full dark. The narrow stream was still frozen over, but the ice had become a leaden gray.

"More of this warm weather, and it'll be thawed through," said Mac.

"Reckon it'll change, Dad?"

"Could be, John. See if the wind starts veering back northerly. It carries snow from Canada in its teeth when it does."

"Look."

Paul stopped dead, pointing at the side wall of their small, shingled barn. It was normally painted dark brown, but the snow was still piled three or four feet high against it.

Someone had come in while they were away on the hunt and daubed a message on the wall in what looked like yellow highway paint.

Think you got the guns so you think you got power well you got a leson to lern abouot real fucking power your all dead.

13

Somebody was calling his name, but his attention was on the road that wound out ahead of him, lined with abandoned churches.

"Jeff, come on now, Jeff."

Each of them had a magnificent stained-glass window overlooking the highway, but in every case the color had leached out, leaving behind weird images of crucified saints that looked like a series of photographic negatives.

"Jefferson!"

It was odd that all of the tortured figures looked like Jed Herne. Jed was dead.

"Dead," whispered Jeff Thomas.

Of course he was dead. He wasn't going to rise on the third day and come to judge... judge anyone. Not on the third day. Nor the fourth. Not on any fucking day. Nobody knew that better than Jeff did. Warm blood on his hand as the knife slid into the flesh. Red blood. The blood in the church windows was like the finest rubies.

"Jeff! For God's sake, Jeff!"

He could smell incense and hear the distant tinkling of a tiny silver bell. "Hail Mary, full of grace, blessed art thou and blessed ... Forgive me, for I've sinned. I've taken life and lied and fornicated ... the fruit of thy womb."

Something hit him on the side of his leg, stinging like a thrown pebble.

But he still wouldn't open his eyes. That would be bad news, bringing the pain flooding in like searchlights.

Jeff Thomas didn't want that, so he snuggled down again into the darkness like a child seeking a few more moments before getting up to trudge to a hated school.

Another jab of discomfort, this time on his shoulder. "Come on, Jeff. Snap on out of it, will you? Please, Jefferson."

The voice was familiar, though it somehow didn't seem to sound quite right.

The incense was stronger, streaming from the open doors of the ruined churches like thick smoke. It was blinding him and circling around him as though he were at the heart of a Kansas whirlwind. There was a small dog at his feet, cowering, and a crazed, cackling old woman, pedaling an antique bicycle through the stormy sky.

"Dorothy?" Why should Dorothy be throwing stones at him?

Finally, very slowly Jeff Thomas opened his eyes. Nothing was in focus, and his whole head and body rocked with spasms of agony. He'd known it was going to be a mistake, so he closed his eyes again. But the pain didn't go away.

"Hell . . . oh, goddamn hell."

The other voice was drifting toward him from the semidarkness. "That's better, Jeff. More like what I want to hear. Stick with that. Screw your courage to the sticking place, Jefferson."

"Screw your courage, Nanci!" That was who it was. Nanci Simms. The Mercedes. Calico ghost town. Earthblood.

Now the memory was inching back reluctantly.

There was a vague impression of being torn from sleep by something heavy crashing into the side of his head. He'd tried to shout, but his mouth had filled with the iron taste of his own blood, and another savage blow knocked him back into swirling blackness.

He'd heard the sound of gunfire, as if from a great distance, but it merged with the noises inside his own skull, to be swallowed by nothingness.

"You all right, Nanci? What the hell happened? Feel dead."

"I'll take those in reverse order. You aren't dead, though I imagine your head must feel as if it was under a buffalo stampede. What happened was that four of the country's great unwashed and thoroughly unlovable came up on us in the dark and did us some grievous harm. And am I all right? I fear the answer is that I'm not particularly all right.''

But Jeff wasn't really paying much attention. ''What happened to the four men? I thought I heard shooting as I got to be unconscious.''

''They got to be dead.''

''Terrific! Serve the bastards right! Great, Nanci!''

''Jeff, can you come over here?''

Now he knew what it was about her voice that seemed odd and unfamiliar.

Nanci Simms sounded weak and feeble.

''You hurt?''

''Some.''

''Bad?''

''Just come over here, will you?'' This time there was in her voice a touch of the old arrogance and power that frightened Jeff so much.

''Sure. Jesus, my head!'' Cautiously he reached to touch the throbbing center of the pain. ''There's blood all over my hair, my neck. Some of it's dried, Nanci. How long since—''

''About an hour. Been trying to wake you. I could hear your breathing, rattling away there like a rutting moose, so I knew you must still be in the land of the living.''

"Dead?"

"All four."

"I heard the shooting."

"So you said. Can you try and come over to me, Jeff? I need some help."

"You shot them all?"

"Managed to reach the Port Royale and stitched them up like pretty maids all in a row. But..." There was a gasp of pain. "Yes, I was just a little slow on the extermination front. Getting careless in my old age."

"They shoot you?"

"No."

"Then..."

"Oh, Joshua, Judges, Ruth! Will you get over here right now."

He stood, swaying unsteadily. Suddenly he propped to hands and knees and threw up. Throat straining, mouth filled with the bitterness of bile. He coughed and spluttered, feeling as though he was likely to choke on his own vomit.

"Don't play the rock star with me," said Nanci in an odd singsong voice.

"What?"

"Filling your air passages with puke, like some of the old-time rock and rollers did. Buying your one-way ticket to oblivion and a sort of lousy second-rate immortality."

"I feel god-awful."

"Sure you do. They say that life is a bitch and then you die, Jefferson."

"Feel like death now."

"They also instructed us to live fast and die young and make a beautiful corpse. I fear that I qualify on some of those conditions."

With a struggle, he made it back to his feet again, blinking in the semidarkness. Now he could see the dead men, lying between him and the silvery ghost of the Mercedes-Benz, sprawled so artistically it looked as if they'd been placed there by a stage designer.

"They got on uniforms, Nanci," he shouted, his voice dropping quickly as he realized how loud it sounded in the stillness.

"Badges?"

Jeff stooped over the nearest corpse, when a hand shot out, clutching his ankle with feverish strength.

Jeff let out a panicked squeal, kicking in shocked horror and very nearly losing his balance again. A lance of white pain burned behind his right eye from the jerking movement.

"Kill him, Jeff," she called out, a note of panicky desperation in her voice, revealing a terrified weakness in Nanci that unsettled him even more than the sudden attack.

As the dying man on the ground muttered a string of curses, Jeff's right cheek was twitching down at the corner of his mouth, making it look as if he was trying to placate the man with a sickly, jerking smile.

With a surprising ease, the Smith & Wesson .45 was in his hand, his index finger on the trigger.

He put three of the eight rounds into the skull of the figure at his feet. For a second the lethal grip on his leg tightened with an awesome ferocity, then relaxed.

"Finished?"

"Yeah, Nanci, finished. Bastard's head must be in at least three hundred pieces."

"You were checking for badges."

This time he was more careful, but the other three were undeniably dead.

"A golden arrow through a silver sun. Least, that's what it looks like."

"Uniforms?"

"Right. Like the ones back at Calico. Kind of semimilitary. Dark blue pants and camouflage tops."

"Sounds like the way Flagg's security men used to look. But he can't . . ."

"Who's Flagg, Nanci?"

"A dead man."

"Then he can't hurt us."

"Dead have long nails."

"Where'd he live?"

"Vegas."

"Not all that far away."

"True."

"When?"

"Not now, Jeff. Come here. You have to help me. Just do what I tell you."

He holstered his gun and picked his way across the uneven ground to where he could see her. She was lying in a peculiarly hunched way, her hands jammed between her thighs.

On the way Jeff stepped over the pair of matched Heckler & Koch P-111s, resting right by the torn remains of her sleeping bag.

There was enough light for him to see that Nanci was bleeding. A pool of glistening blackness oozed from between her fingers. The wound was high in her leg, close to her groin.

"Knife?"

"Long thin blade. Tried to roll and kick it away, but he was quick. Quicker than I expected him to be. I missed." A long, painful pause. "He didn't."

"How bad is it?"

"He got the femoral artery. Guess I'll never know if he was lucky or really, really good. Lost a lot of blood. I'm holding it pinched, but I'm starting to cramp up."

The Port Royale was a yard or so from Nanci Simms's feet and Jeff picked it up, slinging it over his shoulder.

"Put that in the auto. Rifle's there. Get the automatics, as well. Then give me a hand. Think it'll need stitching. I can do that if you can hold it shut. Not too long a wound, but it's deep enough. Let go and it'll spurt twenty feet and I'll be dead in three minutes."

"There might be more of them coming out after us."

"Yeah. Quicker we get moving away from here, the better our chances."

"*We*, Nanci?"

There was a long stillness. Then she said, "Ah, I get it, Jefferson."

"Time I moved on."

"You won't make it on your own."

"I can try."

"Sure. Prince among men, Jeff, aren't you?"

He turned away from her, toward the sports car, feet sinking in the soft mud.

"Mind if I give you a small piece of information?"

"I'm listening."

"I seriously advise you to reconsider. I'll forgive a single mistake. I'll make you pay for it, of course. Pay the sort of prices you like, Jeff."

He closed his eyes, fighting against the insidious voice.

"Not this time. I've liked what you made me... But I'm real keen on living, Nanci. Can't wait around."

"Why not kill me?"

"No need. Desert'll get you, or the hunters. You said yourself you can't move."

She laughed quietly. "Big mistake, Jefferson. Big mistake."

That was the last thing he heard her say as he climbed into the Mercedes. He gunned the motor and slewed sideways, spraying Nanci with dirt, leaving her, with her finger and thumb pressed against the severed artery, alone in the desert.

Jeff headed south, toward Las Vegas.

14

The brakes came on, locking up the rear wheels of the pickup truck and sending it sliding toward the side of the road.

Sly rolled over like a sack of potatoes, his face a mask of comical dismay, squeaking in alarm as he bumped into Heather Hilton.

Jim's reflexes were honed enough for him to brace himself against the juddering skid, but he still nearly fell against his daughter.

The first thought was that they'd blown a tire. The second was that a coyote had darted across the highway in front of them.

"Stay with the vehicle and keep your hands away from any weapons!"

The harsh voice, its order amplified through a bullhorn, gave him the right answer at the third attempt.

"Shit," he said.

There was a long earth-mover, painted sunburst yellow, with two bulldozers, one at either end, sealing off most of the road. The gap at the end, just wide enough to admit a single vehicle, was blocked off by a red-and-white pole balanced on top of a couple of rusting oil drums.

Looking over the roof of the cab, Jim was able to see five armed men. No, there was a sixth one, manning an LMG, mounted on a makeshift platform of bricks and planks.

They all wore dark pants, mostly with quilted camouflage jackets. All of them had a badge on the lapels.

Jim couldn't quite make it out, but from the distance it looked like a yellow dagger through a silver disk of some sort.

"They friends, Jim?" Sly's gentle, round face was worried, and he was reaching out to hold Heather's hand.

"Maybe."

For no reason at all, Jim Hilton half remembered a line from some old poem he'd done at high school: "Nothing they know of friendship, who only friendship know."

Something like that.

The voice barked again. "Don't like saying it twice. Engine off and hands where we can see them."

"He never said that once."

Jim heard Steve Romero's muttered comment. He reached down and touched the cushioned grips of the Ruger, reluctantly leaving it be. The men at the roadblock all carried rifles and looked as though they knew how to use them. They were trapped in the pickup, where any effort to fight would inevitably lead to plain bloody butchery.

He ran his fingers through his thinning blond hair, now well down to his shoulders.

The movement attracted the attention of the man with the bullhorn. "Tall guy on the back of the truck. Stop moving around. Let's see everyone's hands up there, trying to catch a slice of sky."

Heather lifted her hands, dragging one of Sly's arms up with her. "Come on," she whispered.

"Fat kid only got one hand? If not, he better get it up there."

Steve leaned out of the window. "Leave the boy alone!" To his son he said, "Sly, do like they say. See how high you can stretch up. And don't put your hands down until I tell you."

Two men, carrying M-16D4s, eyes bright like hunting polecats, fanned out to cover the vehicle, moving light-footed.

"One at a time. Tall guy on the back. Step over slow and easy. Then the girl and the fat kid. After that you two in the cab. Driver first, last the skinny black in the passenger seat."

Jim felt a flicker of hope. Somehow they hadn't seen Carrie Princip. She must be lying flat between Kyle and Steve, out of sight.

But all she had was a six-shot .22 Smith & Wesson—against six heavily-armed men.

As he climbed down over the tailgate, Jim managed to stumble. Under the cover of tangled limbs he managed to switch his powerful handgun from its holster to the back of his trousers, hidden by his jacket.

"Don't fool around, Jack, or you get to be dead before you get to be dead. Move it, people."

Steve and Kyle stood close together, masking off the interior of the cab from the men with the automatic rifles. Sly was next to his father, but Steve was making sure the boy didn't turn and see Carrie, knowing that Sly wouldn't be able to control himself, wouldn't recognize the danger.

Heather stood next to Sly, her father close by on her left.

The five military types were ranged in a half circle and were now slightly more relaxed. Behind the barrier the machine gunner had lit a cigarette and had climbed down off the platform.

"Now, we better think about some names, people. I got me a list..." The tallest of the group, who was still holding the bullhorn in his left hand, was rummaging through the pockets of a smart combat jacket decorated with what Jim Hilton could now see was a silver sun, transfixed with a stylized golden arrow.

"What list?" asked Steve Romero. "Didn't think anyone was organized enough to have a list."

"Then you thought wrong, didn't you? Because I got me a real good list. You tell me who y'all are, and I'll see if we have you down as being a wanted or a not wanted."

Jim didn't much like the sound of "wanteds" and "not wanteds." It was looking as if things were going downhill fast.

Maybe because the paramilitaries didn't realize they could be a threat, they hadn't been searched for weapons, at least, not yet.

Kyle's Mannlicher rifle was in the back of the truck, but Jim didn't know what the navigator had done with his Mondadori .32.

Steve's bowie knife, strapped to his waist, was in sight. But the sawn-down shotgun was also in the bed of the pickup, alongside the .357 Magnum rifle.

Against the group of men, it would have provided the most effective weapon. Maximum punch at a minimum range.

But Steve had also been wearing a small blued-steel .32 automatic. A very old Beholla pocket pistol, holding seven rounds. Jim wondered just what he'd done with the gun.

The leader of the gang finally pulled out a sheaf of crumpled computer paper and peered uncertainly at it. "Right, got it now." He pointed at Jim. "Start with you."

"Name's Laszlo Kovacs."

The finger, heavily tobacco-stained, ran down the list. One of the other men suddenly nudged the leader in the ribs.

"What?"

"That guy's carrying a big knife. Maybe the fuckers got guns."

"You carrying a gun, Kovacs? If you are, you got one chance to take it, slowly and very, very, very carefully, and lay it in the dirt down by your feet. Same applies to the rest of you."

Nobody moved.

"Don't like that sort of response. You don't have guns, then let's hear you all sing out good and loud! Come on, people!"

Jim was aware of everyone's eyes slanting toward him, and even more aware that Carrie Princip was hiding just behind him, presumably waiting for the right moment to make a move.

It looked to Jim as if this might be about the last right moment they were going to get.

"I don't have a gun, mister," he said slowly and clearly. "If I did, then it'd be an instant condition triple-red, right now!"

The phrase was familiar to all United States space exploration crews since way back when it had meant what Zelig had once referred to, in a rare joke, as an ordure-ventilatory situation.

Carrie reacted immediately to the prompt.

The small-caliber Smith & Wesson revolver seemed to make more noise than a grenade launcher, the sound reverberating in the cab of the truck. Sly Romero screamed and started to fall to the ground, hands going over his ears.

Heather dived for cover, away from her father, scrabbling to get under the pickup.

Steve and Kyle had both been ready, nerves straining, and they both reacted with blinding speed. One of the things that astronauts had was wonderful reflexes. In a flash, each of them drew a handgun from hiding.

Jim grabbed so fast for the Ruger in his belt that he nearly dropped it.

"Machine gun's mine!" he yelled, knowing that there lay the greatest danger. The massive full-metal-jacket .44 would have gone clean through an automobile.

It all took less than three seconds after the crack of Carrie's Smith & Wesson 2050.

In that splinter of time, she had squeezed the trigger twice more, lying prone on the seat, arms extended, right wrist gripped in the left hand for steadiness.

The armed men were taken totally by surprise at the burst of fire from the hidden, unsuspected assailant. The range was below twenty feet, and they were close together.

Carrie's first shot was best aimed, hitting the nearest target through the bridge of the nose and kicking him onto his back. He died before he crashed onto the ground, legs flailing, fingers opening and closing convulsively. Blood was pouring from the shattered rear of his skull.

Her second shot struck the next man through the right shoulder, making him drop his M-16D4 on the highway.

Her third shot knocked the bullhorn from the leader's hands, exploding it into jagged fragments.

The half-dozen enemies were slow to react to the burst of shooting.

Kyle and Steve both emptied their weapons, and most of their thirteen rounds found flesh and bone.

Only one of the paramilitary men managed to fire in retaliation. But he was already dying, going down into the darkness, as he sprayed a dozen full-automatic rounds into the side of the truck, opening bright silver holes in the rusted metal.

The farthest away was the figure by the machine gun, but he reacted slowly to the crimson ballet of death that was flowering before him. The cigarette fell from his open mouth, and he made a fumbling gesture toward his weapon.

Jim took a long, deep breath, holding it in and steadying the heavy blued-steel revolver at arm's length, his index finger settling firmly on the wide trigger.

The spurred hammer clicked back, and there was a frozen moment before the Ruger fired. A moment when Jim Hilton *knew* with an absolute clarity that a miss was impossible.

It hit the machine gunner through the base of the skull as he started to turn away. It drilled upward, already tumbling, then exited through his half-open mouth, spinning his body down to the ground.

Then nobody moved, the men on the ground still in the pools of blood around them, and the survivors in a frozen tableau as if they were afraid to believe that they still lived.

At last Jim lowered his weapon dazedly and looked around.

Sly was lying in the back of the pickup, hands between his thighs, sobbing quietly to himself. Steve and Heather were sitting by him.

Jim was amazed at the way his young daughter coped with the horrors of life after Earthblood.

She'd scrambled out as soon as the shooting stopped, perky as though it had been hide-and-seek at her eleventh birthday party back home.

Steve and Carrie checked out the dead. Since his gun was empty, it had been up to the woman to administer the coup de grace to two of the wounded. She kneeled without a moment's hesitation beside them and pressed the muzzle of the warm .22 to the backs of their heads, near the left ear. The shots made the bodies jerk before they sank into final stillness.

"You did real good, Carrie," said Jim, reloading his own revolver. "Brilliant. If there was a government to recommend you to, then I'd...well, I'd recommend you for the finest medal."

"Thanks. The rest of you did good, too."

"Pretty well. But you, Steve," he said, raising his voice, "and Kyle. Try not to leave yourself with an empty gun. Count your shots and save one. Never know what you might need it for."

"Yeah," said Steve. "Sorry." Kyle simply nodded his agreement.

"I can't believe that I had to put them out of it," Carrie said, shaking her head. "Both men had about four bullets in them—and they were still living."

"Life's not like the vids, Carrie," said Jim. "Never was."

He stooped and picked up the fluttering pages of the computerized list from where it lay, sodden in the spreading pool of blood by the clawed hand of the leader.

It was mainly page after page of names, broken up into what looked to be arbitrary sections, some with only three or four people identified on it. Most sheets carried the superscription "Not Wanted."

The last couple of perforated sheets were marked "Wanted." A further notation stated "Refer to HoSHQ. Attention F."

"Look," said Carrie, pointing with the four-inch barrel of her Smith & Wesson.

The gun was touching the word "Aquila."

Beneath it was an alphabetical list of all the crew's names, beginning with Cortling, Marcey, ending with Turner, Peter.

"Least somebody wants us," breathed Kyle.

Jim Hilton clicked the full cylinder into place on the Ruger. "Let's move out," he said.

15

Nanci Simms had forgotten more about survival techniques than most people ever learned.

The best way to die was to do something stupid, like leaving your vehicle in the desert and wandering off into the wilderness. But she also knew that you could do everything correctly and still get dead.

She lay back and listened to the sound of the Mercedes's powerful engine fading away across the endless stillness.

"Bastard," she said with a gentle venom.

As the day advanced, every now and again she eased her grip on the deep arterial wound in her thigh for a second, looking down with a dispassionate interest as a bright crimson trickle immediately appeared between her fingers and thumb. It flowed smoothly down her leg, into the hot, thirsty sand.

"What they used to call a catch-22," she whispered.

If she lay where she was, then she would be dead of dehydration within a few hours. The brains in her skull would finally begin to bubble like gray-pink oatmeal once the body's temperature regulator gave up the unequal struggle.

Night wasn't that far off, and the woman guessed she could live that long. Probably through into the middle of the following day.

If she tried to move, she'd be unable to keep a grip on the knife wound, and the blood would gush out like a scalding geyser. She would be unconscious in less than three minutes.

It was a catch-22, all right, but she wasn't ready to give up.

Shade and fluids, those were the two vital ingredients in staying alive in a desert environment.

The former wasn't impossible. There was a pile of tumbled boulders of Navaho sandstone only a few yards behind her. Nanci knew that if she was exceedingly careful she could crawl to its scant shelter without hemorrhaging.

Fluids, her weakened mind whispered to her. She needed fluids, to guard against the dehydrating heat and at least compensate a little for what blood she'd already lost.

From where she was lying, she could see the glint of metal at the belt of one of the corpses. She squinted against the harsh sunlight, making out the shape of a round metal canteen half beneath the stiffening body.

Nanci drew in several long slow breaths, listening to the silence. The only sound was the buzzing of large brown-speckled flies that had been attracted by the exciting odor of fresh blood.

Her light blue eyes opened and closed. "Well, old girl, there is no time like the present. Or there'll be no time at all." She laughed, a harsh sudden noise in the stillness. "Well, they say gallows humor is always a help."

The heat was beginning to get to her, and the temptation to lie still was almost overwhelming. But she could feel the tightness across her forehead and a slight fuzziness fringing across her mind.

"Now," she said.

THE ROADS WERE surprisingly clear.

Jeff was able to set the cruise control at seventy-five miles per hour. He relaxed, feet off the pedals, hands gripping the pale leather of the steering wheel. The air-conditioning was full on, blasting a stream of icy air toward his face. Around him he was conscious of the baking desert air flowing past him in the sports car.

Occasionally he spotted some obstruction in the shimmering ribbon of heat-distorted blacktop. Then he touched the brake, dropping out the cruise control, immediately giving him back total command over the powerful Mercedes.

This time it was a coyote, grizzled, its fur sparkling with streaks of silver gray, its questing muzzle turned toward the approaching car. Jeff was about to tap the horn when a sense of caution overcame him. Instead, he gunned the motor, aiming directly at the animal.

At the last moment it scurried away onto the sandy shoulder of the highway, jaws open, almost as though it was laughing at him.

Jeff swore and swung the wheel farther, hoping to be able to clip the coyote with the front fender, but it was too quick.

The blacktop was covered in a film of blown dirt, and the back end of the sports car started to slide as he sawed angrily at the wheel.

The rear wheels came off the pavement, kicking up a plume of orange dust. The nose dipped, making the whole car jolt and shudder. Jeff didn't have time to worry about what was happening. Split seconds later and he was snaking back down the road, coughing as he recovered control.

A mile or so down the line and he was sailing again, singing one of his favorite songs from before the *Aquila*'s flight.

The cruise control was on, the afternoon was closing in toward evening, and everything was right with Jeff's world.

NANCI WASN'T SO WELL.

She'd crawled slowly, crabwise, trying to stop her lifeblood from leaking into the dirt, and retrieved the canteen she'd spotted earlier. It was three-parts empty.

The effort of making it to the partial shelter of the pile of rocks nearly made her pass out. "No," she muttered through gritted teeth. "I will not yield."

The wave of dark nausea slithered reluctantly away from the sixty-year-old woman.

If she fainted, then she would let go of the artery. And goodbye would be all she wrote.

"WHAT THE HELL—"

The cruise control had suddenly kicked itself out, dropping the engine revs and allowing the digital speedometer display to begin steadily falling down the scale.

Jeff pressed his boot onto the gas pedal, feeling the surge of raw power pushing him back into the leather bucket seat.

"Better," he said, and smirked. For the first time in over an hour he thought about Nanci Simms.

By now she was probably dead. The witch-queen's, bitch-queen's heart would finally have stopped beating, and Jeff could stop feeling scared of her.

That was good . . . mostly good.

The cruise control clicked out again, and the car began to slow. Jeff's mind was filled with dark memories and he hardly noticed, automatically stomping down again to send the Mercedes roaring up the long incline ahead of him.

The air-conditioning didn't seem so wonderfully chilled. He put his hand out, over the narrow black grille, feeling the cool air on his palm. But it wasn't cold the way it had been. It was almost warm.

Now the speedometer was dropping again, down to fifty miles per hour, though he was pushing the pedal right to the metal.

"Come on," he breathed, feeling the first pricklings of panic touching the long hair at the nape of his neck.

The speedometer showed forty, and now the air was hot, hot as the blistering desert around him.

Jeff stamped down, allowing the pedal to come up, then pushing it to the floor, aware that it felt soggy, like treading hard into a thick layer of spongy, wet moss.

Then the speed dropped down to twenty-five.

Jeff's technical knowledge could have been written large on the head of an average-sized pin. If your car broke down, you called the garage, where some spic mechanic with a name like Vinny would make it work again. Out with the laser cred-card, and you were back on the highway once more.

Ten miles per hour, the engine barely whispering.

He relaxed, whistling softly between his teeth. One of the things that Jefferson Lee Thomas had learned in the past few months was that there wasn't much point getting ant-shit angry when things had slipped out of his control.

The sleek car rolled finally to a halt, the noise of the motor dying away.

Jeff applied the handbrake, feeling it lock tight. He reached and turned the key again in the ignition, knowing in his heart that it was a hopeless gesture. There was a harsh rattling sound, metal clattering on metal, showing not the least sign of starting up the engine again. Jeff leaned back in the seat.

Away to his right the sun was beginning to set, its orange fire surrounded by banks of ominous dark purple clouds.

NANCI LOOKED at the 9 mm Heckler & Koch automatic that rested across her lap. It had been an additional struggle to pick it up, but now she had the means of choosing the manner and time of her own passing.

Twice in the past hour she'd suffered agonizing cramps. A barbed band of white pain had tightened around her stomach, making her cry out in shock, her fingers slipping from their hold on the deep wound in her thigh.

Nanci knew enough about her own body to be certain that she was losing the struggle. Losing it more quickly than she'd hoped, with the specter of dehydration cracking her tongue and blurring her vision.

The precious drops of water in the canteen were eked out with the certain knowledge that the next morning would see the end of the line.

With evening closing in, Nanci had forced herself to scrabble painfully from the heap of rocks toward the corpses.

There were few things that Nanci Simms wasn't prepared to do, but even she winced with repugnance at applying her teeth to the throat of the first of the dead men. She bit and chewed at the ragged flesh, until salt blood came stickily between her lips. She nearly puked, but fought for control.

Sucking avidly at the wound.

JEFF WALKED stolidly south.

He'd taken care to fill a pack with some dried meat and a gallon of drinking water. The Port Royale hung from his shoulders, with extra ammo in the rucksack. His Smith & Wesson 4506 with the five-inch barrel and wraparound Delrin stocks was on his right hip. A supalite sleeping bag was strapped to the top of the pack.

It was growing dark, and colder.

BY DAWN, things had changed drastically for both Jeff Thomas and Nanci Simms.

Things were very different.

Yet they were oddly very much the same.

16

"Happy birthday, dear Pamela, happy birthday to you."

Henderson McGill clapped his hands together, face flushed with an amiable mixture of excitement and draft beer from the cellar. "Come on, come on. How 'bout three cheers for the birthday girl?"

His oldest son, John, pounded on the oak refectory table. "Hear, hear, Dad! Three cheers now for the best little sister in the whole of the goddamn brave new world!"

The entire family joined together, celebrating the eighteenth birthday of Pamela McGill, third of the six surviving children.

It was early evening, midNovember, up in Connecticut. A steady fall of snow had begun the previous night and had laid down a blanket of nearly six unbroken inches. Mac had been out with his two oldest sons around noon, all well armed, checking that nobody had been sneaking around their land. But the perfect whiteness was unsullied.

Jack, nearly seven, was sitting on the massive Victorian oak sideboard, drumming his heels together while he joined in the cheers for his sister. As he waved his arms around, the boy very nearly dislodged the print of Edward Hopper's *Nighthawks* that hung on the wall. His mother, Angel, waved a finger in stern warning.

Despite the difficulties of their isolation, caused by Earthblood, everyone had managed to find a present for Pamela.

Jeanne, her mother, had given her a small platinum ring, set with a tiger's-eye stone, that had belonged to her own mother. Angel had rummaged in her possessions for a cameo brooch on a thin chain of golden links that had been a wedding present ten years ago from Mac's mother.

John had carved a tiny goat from a lopped piece of apple wood.

Paul gave Pamela a somber black Apache tear, polished until it gleamed, set in a small box of maple with a glass top.

Jocelyn, Jack and Sukie had worked together, helped by their mother, to produce a collage picture, drawing on the shoe boxes of family photographs that lay in the closet beneath the stairs.

Mac had given a lot of thought to what he could give his daughter. Finally he settled on a fine illustrated edition of the poetry of Robert Frost, which had been a gift to him on his own eighteenth birthday from his old English teacher, Carla Wright. It was something that he'd always treasured.

The two women had spent hours browsing through the larders among the makeshift shelves of potted and preserved foods, trying to find something that might somehow bring back the flavor of the old birthday parties.

"Listen to us, Mac," Jeanne had said, "talking about 'old' birthday parties. Like they happened a century ago."

"It was more than a century," he'd replied. "It was a lifetime back. It's only a year or so since the old times. But they're never going to come back. Not ever."

There'd been venison, a whole haunch cooked over an open fire in the backyard, though Mac and the two older boys had been concerned about the smell of the roasting meat attracting bad company.

Canned vegetables were offered with the roast, followed by an assortment of pies and pastries. Some fresh bread with almost the last of their shrunken supply of precious butter was also put on the table.

Angel had baked a beautiful cake, rich with dried fruits and marzipan. The only container large enough in the house for all the ingredients was the blue-and-white porcelain bowl from the bedroom.

It dated back into the eighteenth century, carried by Mac's ancestors from Scotland. The blurred outlines of the ancient flowers and thistles were barely visible on its smooth sides. Now it stood to one side of the sideboard, dangerously close to where Jack was perched.

The cake was ornamented with multicolored icing. Pamela's great love had always been reading, so Angel had made a pile of books from the sugary marzipan, setting them on a green grassy bank with a vivid blue stream flowing by.

"Time to cut the cake," said Mac.

"Yeah," chorused Paul and John. "Let's hear it for the cake."

"So beautiful, so rich," breathed Jeanne.

Pamela, eyes sparkling, stepped forward to the cake, holding a long butcher's cleaver in her right hand. She'd told everyone that she wasn't going to dress up, not even for her own eighteenth birthday, and wore denim dungarees. But the cameo brooch glittered on one of the straps, and the tiger's-eye ring shone on her left middle finger.

All around the cake, on its large turquoise plate, lay the detritus of the extraspecial meal. The ragged side of venison, dried bones thrusting through the frayed remains of the rich, dark meat. A bowl of buttered carrots, pallid grease congealing on its edges. The white sauce, flavored with nutmeg, now crusted and cold.

Mac wondered for a moment whether they should have cleared the table to give extra pride of place to the beautiful cake.

But it was too late now.

"Too late," he whispered to himself.

A few minutes ago he'd been distracted from the gift giving by the sound of a dog barking furiously a couple of hundred yards north, toward the frozen creek.

Now it had stopped, and the New England evening was totally silent.

"Make a wish as you cut it, honey," said Angel. "But don't tell anyone what it is, or it'll never come true."

The metal blade of the broad knife touched the green icing, near the pile of marzipan books.

"I wish..." Pamela began teasingly, her eyes closed, a half smile on her lips.

A wrenching of metal broke the expectant quiet. The heavy security shutters were torn off the east window of the room, and a Molotov cocktail hurtled through the glass to explode against the sideboard.

Flaming gasoline sprayed everywhere, covering the screaming figure of young Jack.

Simultaneously there was an enormous thundering blow against the front door, cracking it off its hinges. A shotgun was fired through the broken window, the starring lead catching John McGill through the throat, tearing his neck apart and rupturing his windpipe.

His blood splattered across the room, into Pamela's face, patterning the untouched icing of her cake with streaks of crimson.

"Guns!" Mac yelled above the screaming. "Get the guns!"

Jack, his clothes ablaze, had fallen from the sideboard and was running toward the hall. Angel grabbed him and flung him bodily to the floor, covering him with her body and beating at the flames with her bare hands.

It was a world of noise and fire and hideous violence.

Despite the appalling and unexpected carnage, the family had been well trained.

Jocelyn and Sukie had both dived under the dining table to lie sobbing alongside the thrashing, dying body of their half brother.

Effectively there were only four adults to try to repel the attackers: Mac, Paul, Jeanne and Pamela herself.

There were figures struggling to push aside the broken door and gain access through the hall. A window on the far side of the house had been broken, and Mac could smell more smoke.

In a moment of dazzling clarity he realized that it was all over.

Whatever happened in the next couple of minutes, life at the white frame house on Melville Avenue, Mystic, was finished.

"Take out the father!" shouted someone from the back of the building. It was a woman's voice, hoarse and flooded with anger and vicious hatred.

Mac was heading toward the hallway, intent on getting his own Brazzi shotgun. He ran past the blazing sideboard, slipping in the spreading pool of his oldest son's blood, when he became aware of movement behind him, by the smashed window.

There was a man in a fur hood, his head and shoulders halfway through the broken casement. He was holding a blue-steeled automatic in his right hand, leveling it at Jeanne, who was near the doorway.

Without breaking stride, Mac swiveled and picked up the heavy blue-and-white porcelain bowl, then heaved it as he would a discus. It sliced across the room and exploded in the man's face, driving jagged splinters into his eyes.

Before he could begin to scream in blinded horror, Mac had jinked sideways, plucking up the blood-slick hilt of the cleaver where Pamela had dropped it. He grabbed at the greasy hair of the yelling man, making his neck taut, the tendons standing out like harp strings.

He cut the throat with a single savage blow, then vaulted the corner of the table and reached the hall.

The attack had been far better organized than the previous raid against them by mad Preacher Casey. But the work that Paul and John McGill had put in to strengthen doors and windows had thwarted the outsiders.

The front entrance was a congested shambles of splintered wood and twisted steel, with fully half a dozen men fighting to get in. But Mac's five-round pump-action Brazzi rested on the antique settle in the hall with one of the Winchester Defender 1700s alongside it.

Mac's face was a distorted mask of blind hatred and rage, lips peeled back off his teeth in a feral snarl.

He grabbed up the blued-steel Brazzi and emptied it into the doorway. Dropping the shotgun without even glancing up to see what carnage the powerful shells had done, he snatched up the Winchester and fired off all eight rounds. He went on pulling the trigger again and again, even though the hammer was clicking on an empty chamber.

He wasn't aware of the shooting in the room behind him, blanking his mind off from the screaming and shouting, not even realizing that all of the noises were fading away.

All he could see was his youngest son enveloped in a golden hail of fire, and John, his firstborn, tumbling to the floor, arterial blood gouting over the fresh icing of the birthday cake.

Mac could see both scenes, repeated and repeated in his mind's eye.

Then a voice reached him, high and thin with pain.

"Dad!"

In front of him he saw a jumbled pile of meat. Raw and bloody.

"Dad! Stop it!"

Now the voice was familiar enough, though changed. Pamela. The birthday girl. He'd never heard her voice sound like that...on the edge of some undefinable terror...a voice from a nightmare.

Mac kept the pump-action Winchester going, squeezing the trigger time after time. He wasn't taking any chances on anyone trying to get in...into his home...and harming his family.

"They've gone." Tears were in her voice. "Please stop, Dad. The gun's empty."

He moved his feet, aware that he was standing in blood.

A pool of blood.

A lake of blood.

Blood still oozing from the mountain of meat jammed in the front door of Melville Avenue, Mystic. Meat that contained sections that were almost human. A hand, and a portion of scalp. A severed foot, still in a hiking boot. A knife with its blade broken in a jagged edge of steel. A segment of flesh showing splintered ends of ribs.

The hammer clicked on the Winchester.

Mac felt a hand touch his arm, and he jumped, barely resisting the temptation to smash the butt of the gun into his daughter's face.

"Pamela?" he said, voice hoarse and strained, bringing the realization that he'd been yelling at the top of his voice since the first bomb came crashing into the party.

"It's over, Dad."

"You can put the gun down now, Jim. Down. It's over."

A new voice, Angel, standing in the doorway to the living room. Smoke was wreathing out into the bitter cold of the hall. Mac noticed that his wife was trembling, holding up her hands as though she was surrendering to some unseen enemy. Great blisters across her palms and fingers were leaking watery threads of crimson.

"John's dead," said Mac, nodding. He dropped the empty Winchester into the dark puddle around his feet. "And Jack?"

Jeanne was at his side, her arm around his shoulders. "Swallowed fire. Inhaled the flames. The rest of us are...oh God, we're here."

Mac did a quick recon of the house and the yard. Four of the corpses that lay ragged around the house were recognizable as local people. Two were the Baptist minister and his wife.

The rest were strangers.

THE DAY AFTER the burials of John and his younger brother, the McGills held a family council.

"Tainted with too much death," said Mac. "Thought this would be a safe place. We took our precautions, and it wasn't enough."

"We've done the repairs. Doors and windows are safe again, Dad."

He looked at Paul, now the oldest of his four children. "Safe for now. Sure. But what about the next time?"

"Should we try and wait out the winter? Move at the first real thaw?"

Angel's hands were wrapped in strips of clean linen and bound with plaster. Her face was pale, the tangled blond hair scraped away from her eyes.

Henderson McGill shook his head slowly. "No. They've tried twice. Taken hits. But they know we're weaker. Before the end of the snows, they'll get desperate and that could be it. We'll move out at dawn, day after tomorrow. Everyone agree?"

Nobody moved or spoke. He laughed quietly. "Well, nobody disagrees. Day after tomorrow, then. At dawn."

17

"North of Bakersfield."

"That Pine Mountain to the east?"

Jim Hilton squinted at the rising sun. "Yeah, guess so."

"What's that?" asked Sly, pointing north. "Like stars shining."

"Sun off glass," said his father. "A lot of it, too."

They were moving away from Bakersfield, toward Porterville, up on Highway 65, a deserted two-lane blacktop.

Carrie Princip appeared at the side of their pickup. They'd stopped near a narrow stream running between what would once have been banks of delicate feathery tamarisk and taller aspen. Now it was all ruby-stained husks. But among them Jim had noticed the first springing signs of a fresh, hopeful green.

The water had provided them all with drinking and washing. Carrie's long blond hair hung to her shoulders, glistening and damp. She smiled at Jim and he responded with a grin, the shared knowledge arching between them.

The previous night they'd made love....

Jim HAD BEEN TRYING to raise Joe Sirak with the small radio, but he picked up only the ominous soft hissing of uninterrupted static.

Finally he switched the set off and laid it on his blanket.

"Think he's all right?" asked Steve. "Could be lots of reasons he's not answering."

"Sure." He paused. "Lots of reasons."

With their evening meal over and done with, they looked to bedding down for the night.

Sly and Heather slept in the bed of the truck, safe from any creeping or crawling things. It had been a long and heavy day, and the children both dropped off quickly.

Steve chose to lay out his bedroll underneath the pickup, wanting to remain close to his son. They'd already found out that Sly wasn't at his best if he woke suddenly and found himself a stranger in the strangest of lands.

Kyle elected to sleep along the front seat, pushing the steering wheel up out of his way. He coiled his slender length up in the cramped space, grinning at Jim as he closed the door.

"Grapefruit juice and the open-eye breakfast with eggs over easy and Canadian bacon with rye toast. A wake-up call at nine . . . and coffee strong enough to float a horseshoe. Thanks."

That left just Carrie and Jim, sitting together by the smoldering remains of their cooking fire as the stars wheeled overhead.

"Turning in, Captain?" she asked him, leaning across to touch him lightly on the arm.

"Yeah. Looks like a soft patch of sand there, just by those rocks."

"Out of sight of the pickup."

"Yes." He looked puzzled at her comment. "You reckon there's some sort of danger?"

Carrie laughed, shifting to sit closer to him, so he could catch the subtle scents of her body. "Depends on what you mean by danger, Jim."

Now he could suddenly read the subtext and knew what she meant.

"Not long since I lost Lori, you know."

"Yeah. But in some ways it's been around two years, hasn't it?"

"Suppose so."

"So?"

Jim looked at the pale blur of her face, then ran his fingers down her cheek. "I'd really like to, Carrie. But . . ."

She took his hand and moved it to the soft swell of her breast, letting him feel that she wore no bra, the nipple hardening against his palm.

"No 'buts,' Jim. And no...what would Zelig have called it? No 'emotional spillage' tomorrow, either. All right?"

The desert night was cold, but they zipped the two quilted sleeping bags together, snuggling close. Jim stripped naked, but she kept on her pale blue bikini pants.

He was quickly ready. Almost too quickly, and he had to force himself to remember the manual for field repairs on the *Aquila*'s sewage disposal system to stop himself from ruining the moment.

His hand was between her thighs, fingers sliding under the elastic of her pants, finding her warm and ready for him. Carrie's breath was coming faster, and she cupped him in her right hand, her left hand touching his lips.

"Yes, Jim. Now...please."

He gasped as he entered her, the sweet familiarity flooding back to him, aware of her tightening around his body, her arms holding him to her. Her tongue was fluttering at the side of his neck, her breath hot against his skin.

Carrie was whispering in his ear, half-heard words that he could hardly believe. Bedroom words that roused him to a diamond-cutting hardness and brought him rapidly to the brink. But he could feel the woman's stomach muscles butterflying as she raced inexorably toward her own climax.

It wasn't quite simultaneous, but twelve years of sexually active marriage had taught Jim Hilton that it rarely was.

The second time took far longer.

Carrie started by sliding down into the deeps of the double bag, lips and tongue brushing over Jim's chest and across the flat muscular wall of his stomach. Her soft mouth closed around him, and she quickly roused him to readiness.

"That's...that..." he panted, hips thrusting up, fingers tangling in her long hair as he pulled her closer to him.

But before he could come, Carrie had eased herself away.

"No," she whispered, voice rasping with her own need.

"No?"

"Do it for me."

For a frozen moment Jim didn't move. Though the physically intimate side of his marriage with Lori had been largely successful, this was the one no-go area for them.

She would delight in taking him into her mouth, but she would resolutely refuse to allow him to do the same to her, saying that it wasn't right. That woman were "dirty down there." And nothing that Jim Hilton could do or say would make the least difference.

"Not if you don't . . ." began Carrie, sensing the momentary hesitation and unable to conceal her disappointment.

"No," he said. "It's not I don't want to, love. I want to do it for you that way more . . . more than I've ever wanted anything in my whole life."

And it had been all right, better than all right. For Jim it had been the sweetest experience of his life, her giving and taking so joyously, so freely.

Now, standing by the pickup in the bright light of morning, Jim could still taste Carrie on his lips, could still remember the way her thighs had squeezed as she succumbed to the tidal wave of a powerful orgasm, *her* hands tangled in his hair as she tried to pull him even closer.

He looked away from her as he started to feel the renewed tightening of his body, and focused on Kyle.

"Certainly looks like a lot of glass. Some kind of office? Or a school?" Kyle turned again to Sly. "You make out any more?"

"Not like school. Looks like just glass. Me thinks lots of houses built in glass."

"Then we'd better be careful not to go throw any stones," said Heather.

"We'll go down and take a look," Jim said, glancing at the others. "Who wants to drive this time?"

"Me," replied Carrie immediately. "My turn to take control, Jim."

He caught her grin and was overwhelmed with embarrassment as he started to blush.

SLY LIKED THE WORD. He kept repeating it over and over until his father finally told him to keep quiet.

"Highdrypomix," he said one last time with his amiable, moonish smile. "Me like that, Dad."

"Sure, but just leave it out for a bit, Sly, will you?"

Jim had explained to his daughter what the establishment was. They'd parked the pickup a good mile off, in a narrow arroyo, and he and Steve Romero cautiously worked their way through the dead mesquite and sagebrush toward the distant glimmer of glass. Their caution had been merited, as they spotted a number of armed men patrolling a perimeter fence.

"Hydroponics is a special way of growing plants," he told Heather. "Instead of using soil and natural irrigation and sunlight, you put them into containers of liquid that hold all of the chemicals and nutrients that they need.''

"And they grow? Just like in fields?"

"Better, Heather. It's incredibly intensive and... You know what I mean by intensive?"

"Sure. We did it with Miss Kent in the first semester and we..." She hesitated a moment. "We were going to do a project on it in agricultural studies."

Kyle and Steve joined them, with Sly trailing behind, scuffing his feet in the dust, still quietly muttering "highdrypomix" to himself.

Carrie had been watching the establishment from the ridge above them and she came sliding down in a shower of orange dirt. She sat on a rounded boulder, wiping sweat from her eyes.

"That's the future, folks," she announced. "Guess the idea is to produce as much as they can and then gradually refertilize the world outside with the healthy plants. And goodbye to Earthblood."

"Until the next time," said Kyle. "If there's a way of screwing the planet, you can bet your last dollar that scientists'll find a way of doing it."

"Must be hundreds of acres there," said Steve. "Can't have got all that together since Earthblood. The place must've been running for ages."

"And who are the guards?" Carrie looked at the others. "They got some kind of uniform on. Carrying automatic rifles."

"Zelig's men?" Kyle shook his head in answer to his own question. "Not far enough north for that. So I wonder who they are?"

So did the others. The hydroponics establishment fascinated all four of the grown-ups. They agreed that it had to be of sufficient interest for them to try and get close enough for a good look. When they eventually made a contact with General John Kennedy Zelig, they felt he might like to know about the square miles of glass-covered tanks.

"Don't get too near or take any chances on being seen," said Jim. "Heather and Sly can wait together by the truck."

"Let me come, Dad," begged the girl. "It's not dangerous."

"Might be."

"Could be safer to take the kids with us," said Steve. "Suppose they got wide-ranging patrols. Pick them up and nobody here to protect them. We stay quiet and careful, then there won't be any danger. I'll take Sly. You take Heather. Carrie and Kyle can come in from a third vector."

Jim was reluctant but agreed to investigate come nightfall.

There was a bright sliver of moonlight as they left in three pairs. Kyle and Carrie, in dark clothes, went to the right. Jim and Heather took a longer route to the left.

Steve, with the excited Sly in tow, picked the direct line over the ridge and along a wide draw, then into some dead brush. That should give them cover to within less than fifty yards of the nearest of the rows of long buildings.

THERE WAS the distant hum of a powerful generator with forty or so clusters of lights placed around the perimeter of the base. There were fewer guards, but Jim had counted at least five of them patrolling at a steady walk close to the lamp towers.

He was surprised that it was so relatively sparsely protected, assuming it was as important as he supposed it was.

Jim was walking slowly and carefully in the lead, his daughter tracking his steps a couple of paces behind, just as he'd told her.

"Stop, Dad!"

"Shit! You made—"

"Don't move forward."

"What the—I nearly decorated my underwear, Heather."

Her voice was a sibilant whisper. "Something ahead... Saw the moonlight off it. A wire."

Now Jim Hilton could see it, as well—a narrow strip of cable, around midthigh, with two thicker lengths beneath it. Farther along, to the left, almost hidden by a fallen juniper, was an upright post with three white discs on it.

"Electric," he breathed. "Better go back, Heather. Well spotted. Best warn the others in case..."

"We haven't found anything out."

"We already saw with the glasses by the truck that it was hydroponics. Could even read the sign by the main gates. All we're going to..."

Away to their right there was a sudden, startling flash of magnesium light and an audible hissing crack, like the lash of a giant whip.

Jim turned and ran toward it. After a few minutes he heard a sound, followed by Kyle's voice.

"It's me and Carrie. You heard the noise, Jim?"

"And saw the flash. There're high-voltage cables strung around the base, hidden in the brush. Heather saw it in time."

"We never saw that. Think it was..."

The question hung in the cool of the November evening as they stared at each other with fear.

Then from the guarded establishment a quarter mile off, they became aware of a siren, rising and falling like a wounded dinosaur in the last throes of agony.

"This place will be swarming with sentries in a few minutes," said Jim. "Carrie, you take Heather back to the pickup. Get it packed. All our gear. Be ready to move out at ten seconds' notice. Shoot anyone who isn't us."

They didn't argue, running away, feet crackling through the dried, dead branches.

Jim was leading Kyle toward where he'd seen the dazzling flash, when they bumped into the lumbering, puzzled figure of Sly Romero.

"What is it, son?"

"Where's Steve?" added Kyle, at Jim's heels. "Where's your dad, Sly?"

"Me worried, Jim. Me worried, Kyle."

"Where is he?" said Jim, managing with a great effort of self-control to take Sly very gently by the arm.

"Sleep."

"Asleep! He can't . . . Oh, no."

"Me was behind Dad, and Dad fell on a rope and me saw big light and bangbangbang. It was the highdrypomix. Dad sleeping and me couldn't make

Deal Yourself In and Play

GOLD EAGLE'S

ACTION POKER

Peel off this card and complete the hand on the next page

It could get you:

♠ 4 Free books

♠ PLUS a free surprise gift

PLAY "ACTION POKER" AND GET . . .

★ 4 Hard-hitting, action-packed Gold Eagle novels — FREE

★ PLUS a surprise mystery gift — FREE

Peel off the card on the front of this brochure and stick it in the hand opposite. Find out how many gifts you can receive ABSOLUTELY FREE. They're yours to keep even if you never buy another Gold Eagle novel!

THEN DEAL YOURSELF IN FOR MORE GUT-CHILLING ACTION AT DEEP SUBSCRIBER SAVINGS

1. Play Action Poker as instructed on the opposite page.

2. Send back the card and you'll get hot-off-the-press Gold Eagle books, never before published. These books have a total cover price of $16.98, but they are yours to keep absolutely free.

3. There's no catch. You're under no obligation to buy anything. We charge nothing — ZERO — for your first shipment. And you don't have to make any minimum number of purchases — not even one!

4. The fact is thousands of readers enjoy receiving books by mail from the Gold Eagle Reader Service. They like the convenience of home delivery...they like getting the best new novels before they're available in stores...and they think our discount prices are dynamite!

5. We hope that after receiving your free books you'll want to remain a subscriber. But the choice is yours — to continue or cancel, anytime at all! So why not take us up on our invitation, with no risk of any kind. You'll be glad you did!

AND THERE'S MORE!!!

● With every shipment you'll receive *AUTOMAG,* our exciting newsletter—FREE.

SO DON'T WAIT UNTIL YOUR FAVORITE TITLES HAVE BEEN SNAPPED UP! YOU GET CONVENIENT FREE DELIVERY RIGHT TO YOUR DOOR. AT DEEP DISCOUNTS. GIVE US A TRY!

© 1993 Gold Eagle

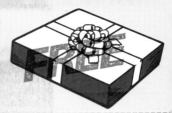

him wake. Shook him, Jim. Me shook Dad. But he stayed sleep.''

"Come on, Sly," said Kyle. "Let's go join Heather and Carrie. Your Dad'll be along a bit later."

Jim walked on, steeling himself for what he knew he was going to find.

18

"Blessed Lord Jesus!"

"May his angels, seraphim and cherubim and all the celestial hosts gather in their brazen armor to protect us."

Nanci's breathing was fast and shallow. Twice in the early hours of darkness she'd slithered away into unconsciousness. But her honed combat reflexes saved her, waking her within scant seconds to staunch the flow of blood from the deep knife wound in her femoral artery.

Now she blinked into the velvet blackness around her, straining to see where the bizarre voices were coming from.

"I believe it is a poor wayfarer, sister, cast away on the drift rock of life."

"Indeed, brother, I concede that you are correct in your assumption."

"Perhaps we should seek to put the traveler away from all suffering, into that bourn from which no man returneth."

Nanci Simms sat up, trying to moisten her cracked lips with a tongue that had swollen and blackened in the desert heat. She gripped the 9 mm automatic in her right hand.

And waited.

THIRTY MILES AWAY, Jefferson Lee Thomas was in better shape.

He was walking steadily toward the south, intent on making some quality distance in the coolness before fatigue forced him to stop and rest for the remainder of the night.

Flagging energy had already made him drink a large part of the gallon of water that he'd taken from the expired Mercedes. Two thirds of his dried meat had also been nibbled away as he trudged along the shoulder of the highway.

There had only been a couple of signs of life on the road.

Once a small roe deer had picked its delicate way across the blacktop immediately in front of him, its hooves pecking at the pavement. By the time Jeff had registered what it was, the moment for shooting it had passed.

The second time it was a pair of coyotes, tails slung between their legs, padding alongside him for a quarter mile, muzzles turning toward him as though they were weighing the lone man up as a potential meal. When he finally stopped and un-holstered the big Smith & Wesson .45, they both disappeared silently into the wilderness, leaving him on his own again.

THE BRACKISH WATER had tasted to Nanci like the finest of chilled Zinfandels, served in a crystal goblet.

Then Brother Edward had held the flickering candle while his sister, Sister Stephanie, had man-aged to sew up the small but deep wound in Nan-ci's leg.

"You have been most brave, dear lady," he said to her.

Edward was in his early fifties, tall and stooped, with rimless glasses and a long beard heavily flecked with silver. His sister was a little younger, with a prominent Adam's apple and a nervous habit of swallowing two or three times in every sentence.

They both wore gray jeans, shirts and parkas, with backpacks. As far as Nanci could make out, neither of them was carrying any sort of weapon.

"We spread the word of the Lord throughout these blighted lands," explained the brother as Stephanie finished binding the stitched wound. Nanci had noticed that he had carefully averted his eyes from her thighs and the pale V of her panties during the operation.

"Now that we have saved your life, Sister Nanci, you are obligated to aid us in our mission." Stephanie rubbed her long-fingered hands together as though something vaguely sticky had come into contact with them.

"What?"

The woman smiled with a wonderfully forgiving Christian charity that Nanci thought made her look like a simpering idiot.

"Yes, of course. Jesus has saved you, so you now become His handmaiden, ready to serve joyfully in apostolic work."

Nanci shifted, aware of the butt of the handgun tucked safely out of sight in the small of her back. "I'm not certain that I wish to devote myself to the Lord. Though I'm awfully grateful to you for your assistance. It was really most Christian of you to help me."

The brother and sister looked at each other. A segment of moon had broken through the banks of heavy cloud, and Nanci could now see them more clearly.

She noted the peculiarly goatlike shape of both heads, with tapering foreheads and prominent chins, and deep-set eyes that seemed to ooze a fervent spiritual love.

"If you refuse," said Brother Edward, "then we shall be forced, with sadness and compassion and extreme reluctance, to blow your fucking head clean off the top of your blaspheming spine.''

"With what? The word of God comes in .38-caliber, does it, now?"

Sister Stephanie stooped over her rucksack and straightened, holding a sawed-down scattergun. "Comes in 16-gauge, does the utterance of the Almighty, you sacrilegious slut."

"KEEP THEM SPREAD, and keep them still.'' The voice had a slow, menacing drawl to it, like a redneck lawman's from rural Mississippi.

Jeff had never seen the patrol. Fatigue had closed down his senses, though he'd never seen himself as much of a backwoods survivalist. His previous idea of a hard time had been getting stuck with the table by the rest rooms at Tante Elizabeth's exclusive eatery in San Francisco.

There'd been a blinding light from a clump of dead saguaros, and then the quiet, deathly voice telling him what to do. Assume the position, flat on the cold tarmac, arms and legs wide, like a stranded starfish on a flat beach.

Helpless.

There were polished boots an inch from his nose, giving Jeff a sudden frisson of remembered excitement. Nanci wouldn't have blundered heavy eyed into a trap.

But Nanci was dead.

The cold tip of a rifle barrel poked him in the back of the neck. "You got some nice hardware, boy. Port Royale, and that looks like a big old S&W there. Why don't you stand up slow and easy and let the guns drop on the highway."

The butt of a rifle grated by his face. Jeff had no expertise with weaponry and he had no idea what sort of gun it was. But he could see that someone had taken the trouble to mark the wooden butt with a sort of brand, neatly burned in the shape of a circle pierced with an arrow.

IT TOOK FIVE ROUNDS from the Heckler & Koch to kill the Good Samaritans, making Nanci even more aware of how kitten-weak she was from loss of blood.

It was difficult to even hold the P-111 9 mm automatic steady and a struggle to squeeze the narrow trigger.

The first bullet had been aimed at Sister Stephanie's midriff, intended to put her down and out of the action and to give time for Nanci to turn her attention to the unarmed man.

But the bullet had struck the stock of the shotgun, tearing it apart into splinters of white wood. The full-metal-jacket round, mangled and distorted, had angled off and clipped the woman on the outer edge of her right hip, snapping a sliver of bone from the pelvis. The force had spun her around, and she'd dropped the ruined gun.

The indrawn breath hadn't yet released her scream before Nanci fired a second round, this time at the paralyzed Brother Edward.

The shot had completely missed him, and the spent round howled off into the blackness.

Then the scream was out and running.

"Shit," Nanci Simms had hissed through clenched teeth, gasping with the cramping pain that was burning at her stomach.

"Die, satanic bitch," Brother Edward had proclaimed in his rich, preacher's voice as he'd pulled a little .32-caliber hideaway from the sleeve of his gray parka.

Nanci had fired the Heckler & Koch a third time, whooping in exultation as she saw the bullet hit the man through the left cheek, blowing away most of the back of his skull, spilling his brains into the dry sand.

Stephanie had tried to run away, one hand holding the bleeding wound on her hip. The fourth round had only nipped at her, taking a strip of bloodied skin delicately away under her ribs on the left side.

It had made her stagger, but she'd kept running, barely visible in the watery moonlight. In another few paces she'd be out of sight.

"Gently, Miss Simms, gently." Nanci had sighted along the barrel at the fleeing figure. "Imagine the trigger is your own clitoris, Miss Simms." She'd remembered the leering grin on the face of the armed-combat instructor at the large complex of buildings in rural Virginia.

She'd squeezed the trigger.

She hadn't risked going for a kill shot. Safety first. Center of the back, presenting the broadest target with the biggest margin for error. High and you hit the head. Low and you still hit the spine. Left or right and there was heart and liver and kidneys and lungs.

It was dead center.

Dead in the center.

Dead.

THERE WERE a number of ringbolts welded to the sides of the open truck. Jeff Thomas was handcuffed to one of them, trying to keep his balance as the vehicle roared along a dirt road, bouncing over ruts, occasionally hitting patches of rippled sand, hard as concrete. The old-fashioned chromed-steel cuffs were so tight that his fingers had gone numb, and he could see a thread of blood, black in the fading moonlight, leaking from beneath the nails.

He'd already learned that there wasn't much use in protesting to the man who called himself Sergeant Sullivan or to any of the taciturn men with him. They all wore dark blue pants and jackets, with the insignia of the silver sun pierced with a golden arrow.

"Just stay where y'are and keep quiet. Your name showed on one of our lists, boy."

Jeff was already regretting giving them his real name. But he hadn't been sure just how efficient their identity filing might be, and Sullivan wasn't the kind of a person who looked as if he'd welcome being told a lie.

He'd been chewing tobacco and had spat it all over Jeff's trainers, standing so close that the ex-journalist couldn't avoid the stink of rancid sweat.

"Now we got your guns and you, too, sonny. Shame that Flagg's no longer with us. That was a dude that sure enjoyed asking questions. 'Specially to folks that didn't know the replies."

"Who's in charge of you now?"

"What d'you do with a door swung open on a frosty day, boy?"

"Shut it."

The man had smiled at him from behind the mirrored glasses. "Then do it."

NANCI SAT on the narrow iron bunk, looking again at the cell. Six feet six inches long and four feet nine inches in width with walls of concrete blocks, painted a pale green. Very recently painted, as there was no graffiti or dirt on them. The door was steel, colored bright, sunburst yellow. There was a small grille in its center, bolted from the outside. The cell had no window.

They'd kept her locked in for nearly forty minutes, and nobody had come to see her. Nanci wasn't that surprised. She'd been taught enough about techniques to break a prisoner, and initial social deprivation was the simplest and most common. Now it couldn't be that far off dawn. Maybe someone might come to interrogate her before noon.

The patrol that had picked her up must have been waiting up on a ridge above the highway, in the darkness, simply watching.

They had come down on her with two four-wheel-drive pickups, each with three armed men, flashing their lights to warn her to pull over in the little green Volvo that had belonged to the dead brother and sister. She'd only gone a quarter mile, and one of the men had backtracked her, finding the two corpses, as well as the bodies of the group that had attacked her and Jeff.

She'd told the men, having noticed their sun-and-arrow flashes, that her name was Veronica Poole and that she was a retired English literature teacher from Fort Worth.

But there were simply too many dead for them to believe her story, so they'd brought her in. They'd been polite and distant, giving her no chances to find out anything.

Nanci had tried to ask where she was and why. And who was the Man? Was it Flagg?

But they wouldn't tell her a thing, though the driver of the truck that brought her in had said that she was obviously a killer.

"And murderers don't live long. They get to be hung real quick."

The cell was temperature controlled, around seventy degrees. All Nanci had seen as she was brought in was a largish building that looked as if it might once have been a high school. With a lot of armed men around it.

She lay down on the plastic-covered mattress, trying to recover some of her strength, feeling the stitches already tugging painfully at the wound in her thigh.

It crossed her mind to wonder just how far Jeff Thomas had got by now.

"I'll bet he's already five hundred miles away from here," she said to herself.

Though they'd searched her, taking away her gun and knife, they hadn't made her remove her polished boots. Inside the right one, snug in a specially constructed sheath, was a slim razor with an inlaid ivory hilt.

It wasn't much, but it was better than nothing.

With that thought in her mind, the sixty-year-old woman closed her startlingly pale blue eyes and slipped easily into sleep.

LESS THAN a hundred yards away, Jeff Thomas found that sleep wouldn't come. The guards left him on his own, though the observation slit opened every fifteen minutes or so and a shadowed face peered in.

But whoever was out there wouldn't respond to anything Jeff said.

Outside, the sun had risen for a bright new day.

19

"I still feel bad about Steve."

"It was just real bad luck, Carrie. Could've been any of us."

"I know, Kyle. But to leave his body out there... I don't think I'd feel so bad if we could just have buried him decently."

It was November 27, 2040.

They were near Devil's Gate Pass, over seven and a half thousand feet up in the Sweetwater Mountains, camped a quarter mile off the side of Highway 395, with a light snow falling around them. Kyle had lit a bright fire of piñon branches, and they had erected their three one-man tents under the flank of a steep granite cliff, giving them some shelter from the blizzard.

Sly Romero was sleeping peacefully, clutching a small wooden manikin that Kyle had whittled for him, naming it "Steve."

They'd explained to the boy that his father had gone away on a really long journey but he'd taken with him a special pair of glasses that allowed him to always keep a watch over Sly and what he was doing.

To all their surprise, the story had been accepted. Sly's only question had been whether "Me speak and Dad hear?" Carrie had told him that he should whisper what had happened during the day, and Steve would be able to hear it all, though he couldn't speak back to his son.

That evening, as in the other nights since his father's death by electrocution, the teenager had infallibly remembered to do as they'd suggested.

They'd eaten their supper of beans and stew, scavenged from an isolated cabin they'd found the previous day. And Sly had climbed cheerfully into his sleeping bag, leaving the flap on his tent wide open so that he could watch the dancing flames of the scented fire.

"And me see feathers from the sky. Dad tell me they feathers from great big bird."

Carrie and Kyle sat close together, huddled inside their parkas against the Sierra cold, listening to the mumbled diary of what had happened to them that day, filtered through Sly's occasional confusion.

"Dad hello Dad. Me had a good time. Pickup went well and me saw lots of not-sleeping dead ones today. Still good gas in cans and me had beans again. That's two times two times today." He giggled. "Me farted lots...and Carrie and Kyle. Not Jim and...can't remember the little girl. They gone off and me see them soon. Me saw wolfs today. Cold, Dad." A note of excitement crept into his voice. "And feathers, Dad. Like you told me. Me saw them. They really called snow. Me know that. But feathers is pretty, Dad, today. Now lay me to sleep and pray me soul to keep. If me die before wake, then pray soul to take. Goodnight, Dad. Miss you."

Carrie looked across at Kyle, the firelight glittering off the tears that streaked her cheeks. "Son of a bitch always gets me every night."

"Yeah. He's holding up well."

"You've never regretted us looking after him? When we split from Heather and the captain?"

"Not for a moment. Honestly. Wonder where they've reached."

"Depends on what kind of transport they found, I guess."

Once they'd made their getaway from the mysterious hydroponics establishment, leaving Steve Romero's charred corpse behind in the scorched brush, the three adults had sat together in urgent discussion.

They had agreed that they should split up to try to increase their chances of locating Zelig and the almost-mythical base Aurora.

The division had been unarguable. Jim would obviously care for his own daughter, but whoever looked after Sly would need some assistance, which meant it had to be Kyle and Carrie.

They'd stayed together for a half day until they reached a fork in the road. One highway carried on roughly northward, while the other struck out toward the west and the ocean. That was the route that Jim Hilton had selected for himself and Heather.

They parted with the agreement that they'd all come together in Muir Woods on December 5.

"There or thereabouts," Jim had said, getting a smile from Carrie and from the tall, muscular black. It had been one of his favorite sayings on board the old *Aquila*.

Now there was only a week to go before the date for the meeting, and Kyle, Carrie and Sly were around one hundred and fifty miles away from Muir Woods, as the crow flies. However, they'd all noticed that there didn't seem to be that many crows flying around the leaden, overcast skies.

Next morning, the twenty-eighth, the wind had risen, blowing the snow cover in powdery heaps, bringing drifts at the sides of the highway.

Sly had trouble taking his tent down, but he stubbornly insisted on battling the flying material himself, refusing Kyle's offer of help.

"Me do it on my own," he said, smiling broadly as he finally managed to get the tent stuffed into its waterproof bag.

"Throw it in the back, Sly, and we'll get rolling on north again."

The boy clapped his hands. "Rolling and rolling and rolling we all gotta roar 'Hide.'"

"Very nearly," laughed Carrie, patting him on the arm.

THEY'D SEEN virtually no hard evidence in all of their journeying that General Zelig was anywhere out there.

But they had come across a couple of hopeful clues, and if there were two, then that must mean that there were probably more.

One was painted in black on the vertical wall of a steep bluff. Carrie had been driving, with Sly dozing in the middle of the front seat while Kyle had been fiddling with a broken camera he'd picked up in a wreck-strewn picnic area.

She'd stamped down on the brake, sending the pickup slewing onto the shoulder in a shower of pebbles and sand.

"Look!" she exclaimed, rolling down the window and pointing out to the left.

The message had obviously been daubed in a great hurry, with paint running streakily over the red-orange rocks.

"Rora North. Z."

That was all.

The second message was longer and just a little more explicit. They found it when they detoured up a dirt road, avoiding a tangled mass of blackened vehicles fused together by a cataclysmic fire and totally blocking the highway. Whoever left the message had obviously driven the same way.

They stopped outside the tumbledown remains of what must once have been a beautiful old frame house. Now the outside staircase to the second floor had rotted and fallen, while the windows gaped glassless and menacingly dark.

"Spooky," whispered Sly, hunching his shoulders protectively.

"Nothing to be frightened about," said Kyle, who was at the wheel.

Carrie narrowed her eyes. "Hold it a second," she said. "Just spotted something."

She jumped down and walked across to the front of the faded, weathered building. The exposed joists looked like old bones.

Her keen eye had picked out something hanging from the battered mailbox. A small flag. It would have meant nothing to most people passing by, but she'd recognized it immediately as the insignia of the United States Space Authority—a circle of tiny silver suns set on a maroon background.

There was a piece of paper wrapped around the thin stick that held the little pennant in place in the box.

"What's it say?" shouted Kyle.

She unrolled it, peering at it, then walked over and offered it to him. "Not too easy to make out. See for yourself."

It was typed on what looked like the most ancient manual machine in all the Americas. The letter *e* was missing, as was the *t*. The lines were irregular, looking like a mule going up a ladder, and were so pale you had to angle the paper toward the sunlight to read them. It was obvious that the typewriter was also lacking any capital letters.

anyon wan s o know abou aurora should con ac caffs groc ri s in wrigh vill nor h of walk r on 395. will b h r un il nd nov mb r. jk z lig.

They were now within only a dozen miles of Wrightsville, north of Walker, ready to locate Caff's Groceries.

WHEN AT LAST the pickup rolled to a halt, they stared in surprise.

"Christ! It's open for business," Kyle said.

All three of them got out of the cramped cab, their breath frosting in the icy morning air. Sly scampered to the rear of the truck, unzipping himself as he ran. Carrie and Kyle looked thoughtfully at the building that stood across from them.

In many ways it seemed like any grocery store in any town, any state, anywhere. Tar-paper roof, single storied, standing alone, with some fresh snow lining its eastern wall. The sign, Caffs, had obviously once been illuminated with a row of light bulbs, but only the broken stumps remained.

The difference between Caffs Groceries and most other stores, before Earthblood, was that it had been turned into a fortress.

Steel grilles were bolted over windows and the only visible door. Inside them it was possible to make out the sullen glint of armored shutters, giving protection against anything short of a concentrated artillery barrage.

There were gun ports cut in the walls, allowing the occupants a range of fire that covered the entire area around the store.

A professionally painted sign was fired over the door, scarred in one corner by what looked like a shotgun shell.

Caffs is open twenty-four hours and 365 days. Knock and wait. A smile greets genuine traders for all kinds of food, drink and weapons. Death greets any robbers, raiders, pimps, scum, whores, dwellers in urban canyons and publishers.

"Why publishers?" shouted Kyle, startling away a bright-colored jay from the satellite aerial on the roof.

The response confirmed his belief that they were being watched.

"Wrote a book once and got screwed by the publisher. Never forgot it." A hearty laugh accompanied the words. "Truth is, not many publishers came this way since the plants started to bleed. What do you folks want?"

"Shells for a .32 and .357. If you got them."

"I got them."

"And for a .22," called Carrie.

Sly had finished relieving himself and was standing with them, staring at the armored building.

"Twenty-two, lady? You aiming to shoot you some squirrels? Do better throwing stones."

"Come out here and say that," she shouted defiantly.

"Maybe not. What you got to trade?"

"Can we come closer?"

"Sure. But don't step any nearer than ten yards. Beyond that and you get dead."

They all walked away from the pickup, stopping at a cautionary shout from inside the store.

Kyle looked around, but the rest of the world seemed deserted. "You heard of Aurora, mister?"

As the silence stretched out, Kyle found his right hand reaching around for his Mondadori automatic. Sly had bent down and picked up a small pebble with a hole through its center, bringing it to his right eye and squinting through it.

"I asked—"

"I heard you."

"Well?"

"You got a name?"

"Sure I do. Why should I tell it to you?"

Carrie had drawn her .22. "How about you telling us your name, mister?"

"Ted Abbey."

Sly had been painfully spelling out the name on the roof, letter by letter. Triumphantly he announced that it spelled "Caff."

The invisible man heard him. "She was my daughter, son. Worked in prisons, doing theater stuff. She went off to England before Earthblood. Haven't heard from her since. Named the store after her. Guess I still hope she's..." The sentence trailed off into a flurry of fine snow blowing around the trio outside the store.

Kyle shook his head. "It's cold as charity out here, Mr. Abbey."

"Names?"

Carrie nodded. "Why not, Kyle?" she said quietly. "Tell him."

"I'm Kyle Lynch and this is Carrie Princip. The lad is Sly Romero."

There was another long pause. They could hear the humming of a generator from somewhere to the rear of the fortified building.

"Son of Steve?"

Surprised, Kyle said slowly, "Right. How d'you...? Ah, I get it, Mr. Abbey."

"Do you, Kyle? Do you? A couple of questions, just to make absolutely sure you're really who you say you are."

"Go ahead."

"You were engaged to..."

"Leanne."

"But?"

"But what?" Anger suddenly started to ride in Kyle's voice.

"But your love was..."

"How the hell...?" Shrugging his shoulders, Kyle decided to go along. "All right. You got the aces, Abbey. It was a lady called Rosa."

"I didn't know that, Kyle," said Carrie.

"I didn't think anyone knew," he answered, loud enough for the man to hear him.

"Zelig knows everything there is to know, Kyle. And then some."

"So. We saw a message you had all the information about Aurora. Tell us."

"I don't know where it is. Zelig made sure only a tiny number of the people involved knew the actual location. That way Flagg and his gutter rats wouldn't be able to get there—not until it was strong enough to hold him off." A brief lull occurred, as if the man was gathering his thoughts. "Anyway, Flagg's dead. But his work lives on." After another, longer pause, he seemed to come to a decision. "You folks best come inside, before you all freeze."

They trudged around the back, and entered through a reinforced doorway.

Then they were face-to-face with the man possessing the voice. Ted Abbey had a neatly trimmed beard, flecked with white, and wore thick horn-rimmed spectacles. His eyes were the palest, milkiest blue that Kyle or Carrie had ever seen.

The moment they were inside the store, he slammed the vanadium-steel security door, locking and bolting it. Immediately he went around to each of the observation slits in the walls to scan the outside once more.

"Fine," he said. "Now we can talk."

20

It was the first day of December.

The armed convoy that was the McGill family had finally rolled and fought its way through to California and was now only a few miles away from the ancient mining ghost town of Calico.

There were three vehicles, all showing signs of wear and tear. Two had bullet holes in their flanks, and the third was badly scorched where an attempt had been made to firebomb it an hour east of Fort Scott, Kansas.

Paul drove an ex-Army jeep towing a fuel tank. It had held twelve hundred gallons when they left New England and was now down to around the four-hundred mark—still more than enough to make them a target for any renegade group they encountered. The cab had been rebuilt using plate steel, and they'd managed to obtain some bullet-proof tires from a military dump less than eighty miles from Mystic.

Jeanne and Angel, whose burned hands were almost healed, took turns driving the second vehicle.

It was a black four-by-four that had started life as an underpowered import from Europe and could now manage one-thirty on a flat, open highway. Jocelyn and Sukie generally rode with the two women.

Pamela traveled with Mac, heading up the fast-moving convoy.

They spelled each other at the wheel of the massive Phantasm, keeping the RV moving along the side roads, trying to avoid any sections that were too steep or winding or narrow. Generally they'd been successful in the long and hazardous trip.

The previous evening, as they camped on top of a high ridge with good visibility for thirty miles around, it had occurred to Henderson McGill how bizarre life had become. That he should think their trip had been *relatively* uneventful.

Several times they'd driven over bloated corpses, not stopping for fear of a trap, hearing the sickening sound of the wet explosions as ripe, putrid bellies burst.

The convoy had been attacked on eight separate occasions, but each time the McGills had come through safely, beating off the raiders with their vastly superior firepower.

Mac had guessed that, on their way west, they'd probably passed a million wrecked cars and trucks and gone within a quarter mile of five million corpses. But he knew in his heart that this was probably a conservative estimate.

Yet they'd been lucky. Nobody had been killed. The only injury had been a sprained wrist for Jeanne while changing a tire.

"Think there'll be anyone up in this place, Dad?" Pamela leaned on his shoulders, her hair brushing against his cheek.

For the fiftieth time that morning Mac checked his mirror, making sure that Paul and the gas were behind, with the four-by-four riding his fender, and that nobody else was in sight.

"Doubt it. We're way late on the date we agreed. But if Jim Hilton or anyone else got there, they'll likely have left us some sort of message. That's what I'm hoping."

"Then off along the yellow brick road to this Aurora."

"Sure. Aurora means dawn, from the Latin, so I guess it fits."

"'Yellow Brick Road' was Jack's favorite song from that old vid, you know."

Mac signaled a right turn and pulled it off I-15 at the sign for Calico.

"Yeah, honey," he said. "I remember that."

At times he remembered too much.

Just before they reached Calico, all three vehicles stopped on the narrow road leading to the town. Mac and Paul stood side by side, looking at the tangled pile of torn and rusting metal, parts held together with what seemed to be baling wire.

"Reckon someone had gathered it after a crash or an explosion and was trying to transport it away. The road bends sharply here. Could be they decided to dump it."

Mac nodded. "Could be, Paul. Think it was an old Chinook. Wonder if it has some connection with the meeting here."

They moved on and found the ghost town totally abandoned. It was obvious that someone had made a hurried attempt to burn it down, but for some reason had abandoned the idea. Two-thirds of the buildings were intact, but there was no sign of any message from Jim or the others.

Once he was confident there was no threat, Mac allowed everyone, including Jocelyn and Sukie, to scout around, making sure every single remaining hut or store was checked.

"Only leaves the half dozen this side. I'll take the—"

"Saloon," called Angel, making everyone laugh. "If Jim Hilton's left you a message, it'll be in that saloon, Mac."

It was.

He found it tucked into a pint beer glass behind the scarred bar.

Jim unfolded it, half watching himself in the cracked and fly-blown mirror. He recognized the writing immediately, feeling a pang of mixed emotions. Part of him wished that he'd stayed with Jim instead of going off to New England to join his families. But thinking about the deaths they had sustained, part of him was also aware that those deaths would probably have been so much worse if he hadn't been there.

Hi, Mac. Hope it went well. Hope you got some of your own squids with you. The more the merrier. We had some trouble here. Way it looks is that Zelig runs Operation Tempest and they have a base code-named Aurora some place north. There are some black-hats called Hunters of the Sun who don't love Zelig and don't seem to love us. So watch your ass against them. We're going to split up and cover as much of the 'north' as we can. I've set a rendezvous for us all to meet at Muir Woods, near Corte Madera, north of San Francisco. December 5. Be there or be square, like they used to say. All good luck, Mac. Your friend, Jim Hilton. Ex-commander *Aquila*.

Holding the note, Henderson McGill left the dusty building and walked out into the chilly morning, finding that the cold easterly was making his eyes water. He climbed to a point where he could see way out north toward the high peaks of the Sierras, shrouded with swirls of winter snow.

Everyone was bone weary from being on the road for so long, from the tension and the long hours and the concentration and the ever-present miasma of death. And from simple fear.

They had to rest a day, check the vehicles, and fieldstrip all the armaments, organize the remaining food and top up the water, maybe on the day after.

That would make it December 2.

Could they reasonably expect to get from east of Los Angeles up to north of San Francisco in three to four days?

"No," he said to himself.

After having survived nearly a quarter of a year since the landing of the *Aquila*, Mac knew certain truths about the blighted land. One of the greatest of these concerned traveling. Main highways were the most likely to be blocked, particularly around the major conurbations where the population had made last, despairing efforts to escape.

To get from Calico up to Muir Woods didn't offer them a lot of options. Mac went to discuss it with the others.

"THERE'S 99 through Fresno. Or 5, but that'll be impossible."

Mac nodded. "Right, Paul. Maybe Barstow and then north up 395. All the main passes are likely snowed up now. We'd have to go a hell of a way beyond San Francisco, inland. And then cut back west and south. Go around Sacramento and—" his finger traced the various options on the Rand McNally "—down the Napa Valley."

"How long's that going to take us, Mac?" asked Angel. "Long while?"

"Yeah."

"We probably got us enough gas, but when you start getting close to cities, the chance of finding any evaporates." Paul looked at the others. "What do you all think?"

Jeanne sighed. "If we leave tomorrow, Mac, roughly how many days?"

"Too many."

"We'll never make it for the fifth. In the old days I guess we'd have done it easily." Pamela bit her lip. "Come on, Dad. Do we go or stay?"

"We stay here and there's nothing. We should try and find somewhere we can winter over, preferably away from the worst of the weather."

"That means desert or coast." Paul looked again at the map. "Muir Woods isn't far from the sea."

Mac rubbed at the graying stubble on his chin. "Right. We go tomorrow, and with luck we can get there close to the fifth. With a good measure of luck."

21

Jim Hilton tugged the hand brake on and switched off the engine, allowing the black van to fall silent.

"The big trees are *alive*, Dad! The first things I've seen that haven't been killed by the Earth-blood thing."

Heather's father wiped condensation off the inside of the driver's window and peered out through the steady cold drizzle.

"Yeah, you're right. I suppose that the simple answer is that the redwoods are so damn massive that the virus wasn't able to survive long enough to wipe them out. Sure is good to see a real green tree. Just like old times."

The winding road toward Muir Woods had been deserted, free of the dumped and rusting wrecks that were a thousand-times-a-day sight on most of the blue highways of America.

THAT MORNING of December 5 saw Nanci Simms waiting to be taken by truck for a final session of examination. The Hunters of the Sun had failed to penetrate her disguise, though they'd pressed her about the names of Jim Hilton and the rest of the crew of the *Aquila*.

Several times she'd heard the name of Flagg as her interrogators bemoaned their ex-leader's death. But oddly she never heard them talk about the person who'd taken over.

There had been a couple of breaks in her questioning when a large camp of squatters and outlanders had been found about forty-eight miles east of the camp. Nanci learned that the security men had terminally wiped the place, hardly bothering to investigate any of the ragged band.

Her own success in concealing who she was, and what she had been, was all relative.

This afternoon, after a final round of desultory talk and some casual, half-hearted violence, she knew precisely what would happen. Because she'd seen it done to others.

A length of thin wire would be looped around her throat, then she would be hoisted onto one of a row of stout iron hooks in the wall of corridor and left to choke and kick out the last hideously agonized moments of her life.

But Nanci Simms didn't intend to go out like that.

No way.

THEY'D PASSED the entrance gates, through the Pacific mist, pulling into the deserted parking lot. Jim had smiled to himself at the way he'd still, from force of habit, made sure that he'd placed the van carefully between the yellow lines.

Heather pulled on her blue sweater and slipped into the fresh air. "Come on, Dad."

He joined her in front of a large notice board that showed a plan of Muir Woods and a little of the place's history.

"How do you say that?" she asked, pointing.

"*Sequoia sempervirens.* Fancy name for the giant redwoods." He turned around to orientate himself. "And that must be Mount Tamalpais," he added, wondering if he'd pronounced it right. "Want to walk a little bit? Stretch our legs."

"Sure. Dad?"

"What?"

"Looks like nobody else is here yet."

"Yeah, it does. Still, it's early in the day yet, isn't it?"

They picked their way along the quiet, overgrown pathways, with the steady, monotonous dripping of water the only noticeable sound.

Finally they reached Redwood Creek and leaned on the wooden rails of the bridge to stare into the white-flecked water.

"Fish, Dad!" Heather yelled excitedly. "Look, loads of them, all jumping."

"Salmon. And those are steelheads."

"Steelheads?"

"Steelhead trout. The way they're going up by those rocks means ... Yeah, we could maybe fix us up some sort of net and trap one or two. They'd make great eating."

Jim shivered as the coastal wind blew through the cathedral of unthinkably massive trees around them. He was possessed by an overwhelming sense of solitude, as if he and Heather were the only two people left alive in the universe.

JEFF THOMAS had decided that he was probably the only survivor from the *Aquila*.

That was what he'd told the interrogators who'd kept at him ever since his capture. Maybe *arrest* was a better word, since there was the total feeling of military control in the way the Hunters of the Sun ran their base.

He'd told them a carefully edited version of the truth, finding out early on that they knew about the crash landing and about the meet up at Calico. So Jeff invented accidents and killings to account for the rest of the crew since that was what the stone-faced questioners seemed to want from him.

He hadn't mentioned Nanci Simms, and neither had his interrogators, which he regarded as probably being a good sign.

But it didn't stop him thinking about her when he was alone in his Spartan cell, lying on his back, hands feeling below the single gray blanket to heighten his own arousal.

It was always the thought of her that set his groin prickling with a hot, disgusted longing.

Part of him was revolted at the pitch of excitement he could reach, thinking about the sixty-year-old woman, imagining her in her gleaming boots, standing astride him....

Afterward Jeff would lie panting in the darkness, loathing himself. No, he certainly couldn't tell them about Nanci Simms. She was dead anyway.

Jeff had wondered about the man called Flagg, who seemed to have been the founder and once the leader of the Hunters. Nobody would talk about him, but it was obvious that the dude was dead.

Also nobody would talk about the man who'd taken over, referring only to "the Chief," with so much awe and fear that it made the short hairs curl at the nape of Jeff Thomas's neck.

He'd been losing track of time, but he thought it must be around December 5.

"WE CAME CLOSE," said Angel, picking shreds of rabbit from between her back teeth.

"Yeah, but close isn't good enough. Doesn't hit the target. Doesn't win the free vacation. Doesn't get us to Muir Woods today." Henderson McGill peered out from one of the windows of the big RV, shaking his head. "Snow's getting worse and worse. If it had just held off for another couple of days, then we might just have made it."

"How long do you reckon it'll be now?" asked Pamela, pulling her dark hair back into a ponytail, helped by Jocelyn.

"God knows. There's three feet on the ground and no ploughs coming through. Could make it in the other two vehicles but not in this. And we need this as a kind of movable home. I expect at least a week...maybe a while longer." He shook his head. "Still, least we all made it through and we're together. Probably nobody up there in Muir Woods anyway."

WAY NORTH OF THEM General John Kennedy Zelig sat alone at his leather-topped desk and looked at the heavily annotated map. There was a small number of special groups of people that Operation Tempest had been trying to locate ever since the violent crumbling of society. People with special talents and skills. The survivors of the crew of the *Aquila* were just such people.

The trouble was that neither Zelig nor his agents knew where any of them now were.

There had been the momentary flash of hope when he'd received the news of Princip and Lynch, with the son of Romero, down with Abbey. One of his very best men.

But the patrol sent down there on December 4 had just reported that Caff's Groceries was a charred heap of cold ashes. There was also a burned-out pickup in the parking lot, and one corpse, believed male, among the ruins.

No sign of any survivors.

THE PLAN had been Flagg's.

He'd originated it, perceiving the ramifications of the Earthblood virus long before anyone else at his level of power. Indeed, the new chief of the Hunters of the Sun had sometimes wondered whether Flagg might not have had something to do with the original release of the lethal plant cancer. He had certainly been lightning quick off the mark.

And now he was gone. Dying, with the greatest of ironies, of food poisoning.

The idea of men and women of authority combining to pick up the reins of the shattered wagon that had once been the United States had been

Flagg's. He'd sounded them out and drawn them in.

Everything was going so well, even better than the projections of the computer program that he had drawn up as a blueprint of what would happen and how they might assume absolute control.

Everything was rolling along, except for Zelig.

If only they could find him and purge his hidden nest. There were other people seeking his Aurora.

"Stupid pretentious name," grunted the chief.

Already they had one, and he would be interviewed by the chief the following day, on December 6. He might tell them something or help lead them in the right direction. It was north. They already knew that.

The chief looked forward to interrogating this journalist. Jeff Thomas.

She always liked interrogating men.

IT WAS MOVING on to dusk in Muir Woods, with a light covering of snow lying wetly around the parked van.

They'd had a meal of dried meat, with a tin of loganberries, washed down with fresh spring water. The last of the bread had been finished the day before. Food was down to subsistence level.

"Still snowing," said Heather, her voice subdued after the disappointment of the long, empty day.

"Yeah. Dark, as well."

"Seems like nobody's coming, doesn't it? Nobody at all."

"Looks that way, love." Jim Hilton felt close to despair. "Yeah, it looks that way."

PART II

22

The snow had stopped falling, leaving the forest around them layered in deep, silent white.

The dry dead branches crackled and popped, sending fountains of golden sparks soaring up into the night sky between the towering sequoias of Muir Woods. The brace of steelhead trout bubbled and hissed on the makeshift spit that Jim Hilton had constructed over the glowing fire, and the scent of their cooking filled the nostrils of the man and his eleven-year-old daughter.

"Never had turkey and sweet potatoes and cranberry sauce for Thanksgiving, Dad."

"Probably won't have any for Christmas, either. Less than three weeks away now."

She nodded, her blue-gray eyes solemn. "Wonder if we'll meet up with any of the others by then."

It was a thought that had been filling every waking hour for Jim Hilton for the past week, ever since the moment that they'd parted company in the Sweetwater Mountains with the other survivors from his crew.

Heather got up to go and scavenge for more wood for the bright-flamed fire, leaving Jim with his memories of the past ten insane weeks. The events, the deaths, the partings, and those of the crew who were missing, swirled around in his head like a bizarre surrealistic dream, making him want to pinch his arm to see if he were really there.

"Nearly made it," he said, his whispered words barely audible over the bubbling of the cooking fish.

When he heard footsteps in the blackness, he looked around, his hand dropping from a combat reflex to the butt of the six-shot Ruger Blackhawk Hunter .44 at his hip, then he shuddered when he glimpsed his daughter. This was how far he'd come with the sweep of events—an unquestioning readiness to shoot and kill, without any thought or weighing of right and wrong.

"It's only me, Dad."

"Made me jump, kitten."

"Dad!" she said reproachfully.

"Sorry, love. Keep forgetting you don't like your old pet-name now."

The slender girl knelt and methodically stacked the armful of wood at the edge of the fire to help dry it out. She was already learning vital techniques of survival in this desolate new world. Jim caught a flicker of his dead wife in his daughter's face, in the way she frowned in concentration. His wife, Lori, buried in the garden of their home below the huge Hollywood sign, his other daughter, Andrea, twin to Heather, lying in the damp earth alongside her.

"You wondering about the others, Dad?"

"Yeah. Kind of running over what's been happening in my mind. Trying not to lose control of any of it. One day someone might want to know all about what went down for us."

His fingers rested in the tangled fronds of dead lichen and some small-leafed ivy. Jim plucked them up and stared at them, seeing the pallid pink color of the dried plants.

"Fish is nearly done, Dad."

"Sure thing. Don't burn your fingers on it."

Heather glanced at her father with a look of infinite scorn. "Been cooking like this for weeks, Dad. Do you think I'm dumb?"

"No, of course not."

He was fumbling with the fish, partly charred and partly raw, when Heather asked, "You think Nanci was really a teacher, Dad?"

Heather had finished her trout and licked her fingers, then wiped them on the leg of her jeans. Jim noticed that it had started to snow again, tiny feathers drifting down through the looming branches of the giant trees around them.

"I think she may have been once. What made you think about her?"

The girl grinned. "I knew you were wondering about everyone. She's the one that seems real odd. You know about her and Jeff Thomas, Dad?"

Yeah, he knew, but he hadn't known that the girl had known—assuming she was talking about what he thought she was talking about.

"Her and Jeff, love?" he said, stalling for time.

"Sure. You must've seen it, Dad."

"What?" His cheeks were beginning to flush at the line the conversation had taken.

"Weirdly weird."

"The way she orders him around?"

Heather snorted with laughter. "That what they call it, Dad? Just ordering around? I seen them two or three times. He was like a slave in some porno vids. Doing everything she told him to. Licked her boots and stuff."

Jim decided that it would be better if he didn't probe too deeply into what his eleven-year-old daughter understood by "and stuff." He also wondered when Heather had been watching any porno vids. But also decided to let that lie.

"I guess both of them could have been chilled by now," he said.

"Won't cry for shit-for-brains Jeff."

"Guess nobody really liked him that much."

"No. Had a teacher in third grade, Miss Leventhal, used to say that everyone had a bit of good in them. Jeff didn't. I reckoned he was the sort of person who was a bully to people weaker than him and a coward with anyone stronger."

"Nanci was certainly stronger than Jeff," agreed Jim. "Fact is, she was probably stronger than most anyone. Can't really believe she's bought the farm."

"Maybe they'll all turn up first thing tomorrow morning," Heather said without much confidence.

"Maybe. And Maybe Zelig'll appear with a chopper to whisk us all to Aurora."

They fell silent in the face of such uncertainties, until Heather said, "Fire's going out, Dad."

"Best get ourselves into the van for the night. Leave the embers to smolder. Won't do any harm, not with this snow starting again."

"What about tomorrow?"

He smiled at the girl, her face only a pale blur in the gloom of the forest. "Tomorrow's another day, Heather," he said.

23

"Poole!" The voice was strident and hard.

Nanci Simms had been dozing after an intensive hour of deep meditation, trying to calm her mind and ready it for what she knew was coming.

"Get off that bed and get yourself to the fucking door."

"Sure." Just for a moment, as she reentered the real world, she had forgotten that the guards knew her by the name of Veronica Poole. The decent, gentle, retired schoolteacher from the northern suburbs of Fort Worth. That was the story she'd stuck to when they caught her and that had been her story through a number of interrogations. In her time Nanci had been examined by serious experts, and what had surprised her now was how little interest the inquisitors had shown in her.

Most of them had been callow young men, who seemed merely to be going through the motions with the questions.

How had she lived since Earthblood?

Where had she been?

How had she gotten hold of her sophisticated weapons? Her response to that had been to plead an old-fashioned, old-maidish ignorance of such things, explaining that she'd found them and wouldn't even know really how to use them.

Nanci was only too aware from her foreknowledge of the Hunters of the Sun that it was all probably futile. They had no need of a single old woman and would dispose of her as quickly and cheaply as possible as soon as they'd carried out their superficial interrogation.

Already she'd seen and heard about the row of stout hooks set in a corridor near an outer wall of the complex and the loop of thin wire that was hung behind the door.

Nanci Simms had no illusions at all about how brutal her passing was likely to be.

The only time that the young man with the pink-tinted glasses caught her momentarily off balance was in the last of the sessions.

She'd been sitting in a plastic chair, lower than the top of his high-tech steel desk. The questioner, his badge with the polished golden arrow glittering through the heart of the silver sun, had been flicking through a large folder, looking bored and somewhat put-upon.

Then he'd casually tossed over a single sheet of paper with stats and photographs of a dozen men and women.

"Ever come across any of these people?"

Nanci had guessed who it was going to be and schooled her face to careful indifference.

There they all were.

Mostly looking younger and rounder than the lean group that she'd met. Their names were printed neatly beneath each picture. Not all of them were familiar.

James Hilton, captain of the USSV *Aquila*. A good thirty pounds heavier and with markedly less hair than the man Nanci had gotten to know. To know and to admire.

Marcey Cortling. Alongside the name was typed: D.O. Landing?

A similar line was next to Michael Man, Ryan O'Keefe and Bob Rogers.

But there was Kyle Lynch and Steve Romero, and Carrie Princip, looking a good deal perter and prettier than the tough young woman Nanci had met.

It had crossed her mind to wonder how many of them were still alive.

An older, harder face. Henderson McGill. The one who had a family in New England and had gone off with the second pilot, Pete Turner. Nanci knew that Jim Hilton felt in his heart that both men were dead.

Jed Herne. Nanci had studied the face carefully, certain that Jeff Thomas had murdered him.

And there was Jeff.

"Think I might know him," she said, pointing at the foxy face with the smug, self-confident smile. "Have I seen him on the vids or someplace?"

"Could be." The man took back the sheet. "Doesn't matter about him. Not him."

As she'd been returned to her cell, Nanci had wondered why it didn't matter about Jeff. Could be he was already dead and they knew it. That made sense.

Now she was going to get chilled.

"Down there. Move it, you old cow. Don't wanna miss my chow."

There were slitted windows, high in the cinder-block walls, and she could just see through them that afternoon light was already fading away.

The guard was six feet six tall, with the physique of someone who worked out with weights. To add insult to murder, her Port Royale machine pistol was slung loosely across his broad shoulders, and one of her pair of Heckler & Koch P-111 automatics rested in his belt.

"Where are you taking me?" Her voice quavered, and terror and bewilderment played over her

features. She let her head slump, hands plucking at
the seams of her khaki pants and dragged her feet
so that the heels of her boots scuffed at the dusty
concrete floor of the narrow corridor.

"Taking you outside."

"Why?"

"To let you go."

"Free?"

"Sure." The brutish laugh gave the lie to his
words. The man was totally arrogant in his sense of
complete power over the cringing old woman.

For a few paces they were out in the open, cross-
ing a patch of dead grass and barren soil. Nanci
glanced around her, trying to get her bearings,
making sure that he was taking her to the isolated
killing passage.

There was what she thought might be a smaller
cell block, with only two or three rooms in it. The
guard unlocked another grilled door, pushing her
into a brightly lit room, then through another door.
Two doors to the left. One to the right.

A second guard was lounging against the wall.

"Hi, Joe. How're ya going?"

"Just got to get rid of this."

"Want a hand?"

The same laugh that made Nanci bite her lip.
"For this? You're jokin', man. Get her doing the
chicken dance and be back ready for supper."

"See you in there."

"Sure."

The door slamming.

A stretch of corridor about thirty feet long. Stark overhead strip lights. One door on the right. One more ahead, heavier, with steel double bolts.

And iron hooks, eight of them, set in the stone wall. The wall and the floor beneath were stained brown and black, and the smell almost made Nanci Simms gag. Terror and pain and death. Something that could never be cleaned away.

"What is this place?" she asked.

"End of the road, slut."

There were two small four-legged stools against the wall. "You said I could go."

"Won't need them stools. Just lift you up and loop the wire around your scrawny neck. Let you dangle."

"No, God Almighty. You can't do that."

"Watch me." One hand scratched his balls. "Yeah, your eyes'll pop out of your ugly bitch head watching me."

"Mother of mercy, this can't be the end of Veronica. Someone'll hear me."

"Yeah. Me and Ed through there. And our special prisoner in his own little room," he said, pointing to the side door. "He won't help. Nor me an' Ed will."

That was what she needed to know.

The door must be to the outside. If the guard had the key, it might work. If he didn't...

And nobody else close enough.

She dropped suddenly to her knees, looking up at the hulking figure with a pleading, desperate expression, hands reaching in a hopeless, clumsy fumbling toward the guard's belt. "I'll do anything," she stammered.

"Anything?"

"Everything. Bet you never been offered everything. I could be real nice for you."

She stared into his face and saw the momentary flicker of crimson lust deep in the tiny eyes.

"No, forget it. Might let you give me a blow job 'fore I swing you. Least you can die happy." He bellowed with laughter. "Die fucking happy."

IN HER OFFICE in the main administrative block, the chief of the Hunters of the Sun wiped her mouth with a white linen napkin, dabbing gently at her lips. She looked at the last few inches of wine in the dark green bottle and decided that she would wait until after the questioning.

It was going to be special.

Reports she'd read of the initial interrogation of the journalist by some of her juniors had tended to make her believe that he truly didn't know much about Zelig and his secret rat hole in the north. But she was equally sure that her own tender, feminine touch might easily open up parts of his memory he didn't even know about himself.

They knew that most of the crew of the ill-fated shuttle were dead. But some had dropped clean off the face of the earth, and Jeff Thomas would certainly be able to tell her all about them. Point a helpful finger.

She laid her napkin on the table and stood up, pressing a white recessed button beneath the edge of the table. "Think I'm ready to speak to the prisoner, Thomas, now," she said when her skinny male assistant pushed his head around the door.

JEFF THOMAS had been sleeping, an uneasy, patched sleep broken by wakeful moments that seemed to have the horrors of nightmare seeping into them. There had been one where he'd been hounded through an echoing warehouse by a gang of young thugs, armed with tiny, pecking knives. It was something that clearly had its roots in the moment in San Francisco when he'd first met Nanci Simms.

The voice of one of the regular guards penetrated his fitful rest.

"Die fucking happy."

There was a small slit in the door where food and drink could be passed through, and Jeff eased himself off the bunk and flattened himself against the wall. He tried to see through the narrow gap, but the angle was wrong.

But he could hear clearly enough.

The voice of a woman. Old and sick and terrified. Begging for her life.

In the short time he'd been held prisoner, Jeff had heard enough helpless victims kicking and thrashing in the corridor outside, and seen some of them as he'd been led out for questioning.

They were some of the nastiest corpses he'd ever seen.

The thin steel wire was looped around the throat so that they strangled slowly, in great agony. The guards didn't even bother to tie their hands or feet. Once they'd been lifted up, or stood on one of the square stools, they were inexorably doomed.

The wire bit in so deep, so quickly, that there was no hope of freeing themselves. In some cases the wire sliced through and burst the artery beneath the ear, sending a fountain of bright crimson to spatter across the walls and ceiling.

He'd never felt pity, just disgust at the stench and mess, and a stirring of panic for himself. But he wouldn't get there, certain that he had something to offer, could make a deal.

Now some old slut was going to get it. But it sounded as if Joe was going to get his pound of flesh first.

"Yes, please, please," she pleaded. "Let me..."

Jeff's forehead wrinkled. Something was vaguely familiar about that pleading voice...

But he was too busy listening.

"So you want it, old hag?"

"Will you let me go...?"

There was the resounding noise of a round-arm slap across the face, followed by a gasp of shock and pain.

"Just get on with it, and no tricks, mind."

The bleak lighting threw a muddled shadow along the filthy floor. Jeff, squinting sideways, could just make out the shape of a kneeling woman, hands lifting toward the towering shadow that was the guard.

"Watch out, belly, here it comes." Joe was laughing and laughing.

Then he stopped laughing.

Stopped laughing very suddenly.

Jeff Thomas wondered what could have happened out in the corridor.

Sly Romero was kneeling down on a blanket, hands clasped together, eyes squeezed tight shut.

The fire was burning brightly, the flames reflecting off the windows of the four-wheel-drive jeep that stood among the trees. Snow had fallen in the past hour, leaving a thin covering over the dry, cold earth.

Kyle Lynch was sharpening a knife on the sole of his boot, and Carrie Princip, left wrist bandaged, sat at his side.

Sly opened his eyes and stared across at them. "Sure it's good me talking to Dad?"

"Sure. Last few days it's been real important we kept quiet. In case the bad men with the guns came up and caught us."

"Like with the fire and Mr. Abbey."

"Yeah," said Carrie. "Just like that. But you can tell Steve about it."

"Did he see it happen? Where he lives?"

Kyle shook his head, hesitating. "Yeah, he... But he really likes to hear you tell about what happened."

"Good, goody, goody good." He closed his eyes again. "You know me was at Caff's Groceries, with the food and all, Dad? Me drink milk stuff, all pink and sweet. Saw pix in dark...liked it, Dad. Things looked good then."

Carrie whispered to Kyle, "Boy's right. Things looked good then...."

THEY'D BEEN HEADING north on Highway 395, toward Carson City, intending to drive the wheezing old pickup westward toward the coast and the rendezvous at Muir Woods on December 5.

A little past Walker, close to Wrightsville, a partly garbled message had led them to Caff's Groceries. The message had indicated they might learn something there about Zelig and the location of Aurora.

Ted Abbey, once he'd been sure of their identities, had warned them that he didn't know where the secret base of Aurora was located, just that it was north. He'd also explained about the threat from the Hunters of the Sun and mentioned their dead leader, Flagg.

"They know about me, you see. Know I'm here. Probably know about all of you, as well. They got ears and eyes everywhere, looking and listening from every mountaintop and every valley. One day they'll come here. Sure I got some good defenses—but I have grave doubts it'll be strong enough. They come with a mob and they'll win. Eventually."

But he'd provided them with good hot soup and some drinking whiskey, thrilling Sly by popping some corn on an ancient iron stove called the Excelsior Dragon.

They'd stayed the night, able to relax for the first time in an age.

Ted Abbey, his white-flecked beard neatly trimmed, had slept in a bunk bed in a sort of open loft. Laying his thick horn-rimmed glasses carefully on a low table at his side, he smiled, the golden lamplight showing his extraordinarily milky blue eyes.

"Now we lay us down to sleep and pray the Lord our souls to keep." Carrie thought he looked like a kindly Old Testament prophet. "Good night, all."

He'd put Carrie and Kyle up for the night on two narrow beds that folded off the wall, and Sly had slept on a sleeping bag on the floor.

When they had risen next morning, it was to find coffee bubbling on the stove and eggs spitting merrily in the skillet. Ted Abbey had gotten Sly to help him by laying the table and keeping the beans stirred in the deep enamel pan.

The boy had been fascinated by the mirrored doors to the medicine cabinet in the bathroom. They were set crooked, so that your reflection vanished as you moved from right to left, reappearing unexpectedly in the other door.

"Sly's gone and back and gone and back," he'd chanted, happily bobbing and weaving from side to side, his grin wide enough to swallow half of Nebraska.

They had sat down together, and Ted Abbey had pressed Carrie and Kyle about their adventures, shaking his head at various high and low spots.

"Why don't you join us?" Kyle Lynch had asked. "Said yourself that the Hunters'll track you down and wipe you out."

"One of these days."

"But that could be tomorrow."

Abbey had smiled, using a rag to pick up the hot coffee jug. "Could be today, son."

IT DID TURN OUT to be that very day. They all heard the jeep coming toward them off the dust-shrouded highway, its engine rumbling, driving a lone coyote scurrying toward the distant hills, belly down.

"Get ready," said Ted Abbey, reaching for a 12-gauge that hung on hooks behind the main door. "Best get the boy in the back room, just in case."

Kyle started to say something, then let the words drift away into the morning stillness as the sound of the powerful engine stopped.

Peering through one of the ob-slits in the heavy security shutters, Abbey reported, "Coupla men. Casual dress."

Kyle had his Model V Mannlicher rifle with the scope-sight, a .357-Magnum round already under the hammer. He was standing by the door, waiting to see how the dice rolled.

Carrie's gun was the six-shot Smith & Wesson 2050 revolver, firing .22-caliber rounds from the stubby four-inch barrel. It was a weapon that had already led to some teasing for her, but she'd proved more than once that it could be the right gun at the right time.

"Yo, inside!"

Kyle had caught Sly's eye and put a finger to his lips. The boy was standing hesitantly in the doorway to the back room of the store. At a jerk of the thumb from the tall, slender black, he went in and closed the door softly behind him.

"What can we do for you?" Abbey had his mouth pressed to the narrow hole cut in the steel.

"Need some food. Got us some good bolts of cloth in the back. Barter with them? Could use some gas, as well."

The sudden opening of the door to the back made everyone jump. Sly stood there, looking worried.

"What?" Carrie whispered.

"Me thought..."

"Can we come ahead?" asked the voice from outside. Neither of the men seemed to be carrying a gun.

"Wait a minute."

Abbey turned to Sly. "Just get the hell out there, will you, son?"

"But..."

"Do it," snapped Kyle.

The door nearly closed, then opened again, Sly's face appearing in the crack. "But me see men washing the wall and roof."

There was a long moment of stillness as everyone thought about that one.

"Fuck!" exclaimed Kyle Lynch, the fastest to react. "Burn us out!"

Abbey leveled the scattergun and fired both barrels at the two men standing halfway between the jeep and the store. One of them went down, but the other threw himself flat. Producing a machine pistol from his belt, he opened fire at the store.

Kyle pushed past Sly, Carrie at his heels, both of them catching the heavy smell of gasoline. There was already a small pool of the dark liquid near the back door, and more was trickling around the shutters.

Carrie was frozen in the doorway, her analytical mind racing over the possibilities, coming inexorably to the only conclusion. "Too late," she said flatly.

"Stinky, stinky," said Sly, wrinkling his nose at the pungent fumes.

Abbey turned to face them, reloading his shotgun, eyes wide. "Best get outside. Only chance if they fire it. Out the front, now."

As he was fumbling with the iron bolts, they all heard the crashing of glass breaking, followed immediately by the sullen roar of flames.

Kyle swung round. "Sly. We're getting out. Run straight for our truck. Got it? Don't stop no matter what you see and hear. Understand me?"

"Sure." Sly was trembling, but he summoned up a brave attempt at a smile.

"Here we go," said Abbey, pulling the heavy door open and stepping out onto the front porch, shotgun at his hip.

Carrie was at his heels, Sly close behind her, Kyle ready to bring up the rear.

The high-velocity round struck Ted Abbey through the bridge of the nose, ripping into the center of his skull. It demolished the back of his left eye, shredding the frontal lobe of his brain. Sight and smell and hearing all disappeared into the darkness.

He dropped the scattergun as the signals went down, taking a halting, clumsy step to his right.

"Shit!" exclaimed Carrie, not sure what had happened, but realizing from Abbey's reaction that he'd been hit hard.

As the bearded man fell, he rolled onto his back. She saw blood seeping from mouth and nose and ears and sightless eyes.

Flames were licking across the polished boards of the floor, racing from the back to the front, making Sly Romero squeal in dismay, pulling at Kyle.

"Two men out front," yelled Carrie. "One near their jeep and one to the right. Too far for my gun."

Kyle jerked himself away from the boy's clutching fingers, bringing his rifle to his shoulder. He centered the cross hairs on the kneeling figure with the machine pistol and squeezed the trigger, then whistled in delight as he saw the man throw up his arms and slide forward on his face as though he was trying to crawl under an invisible fence.

Carrie pointed to the second of the attackers, even as another bullet sliced through the doorway, ricocheted off an oil lamp and buried itself in a sack of dried peas that began to fall to the floor in an endless whisper.

At a range of less than eighty yards, it was an easy shot at the exposed man with the Mannlicher, and Kyle chilled him with a single round through the middle of the chest.

Flames were pouring off the roof as the tar melted, splashing and setting fire to the porch. It wasn't a time for hesitating.

Kyle took the lead, while Carrie tugged at Sly's sleeve, encouraging the terrified teenager to run out into the open. "Come on!" she shouted.

None of them had any idea of what kind of force was attacking the store. The two at the front, both dead, had obviously been decoys while others crept to the rear to start the fire. One of those was also down and done for.

As he emerged into the open, Kyle was conscious of the intensity of the heat from the burning roof. He half turned, seeing out of the corner of his eye that the raiders had also fired their pickup truck, presumably to stop them chancing an escape.

"Kyle!"

Carrie's scream made him spin the other way. A tall man in dark glasses was rounding the corner of Caff's Groceries, holding a chromed handgun. Kyle noticed in that fraction of frozen time that the man wore a blue shirt with the familiar sun-and-arrow badge of the Hunters of the Sun pinned to it.

There was the snap of a small-caliber pistol from behind him, and the man stumbled, glasses falling from his eyes, showing a shocked and surprised expression. Carrie's .22 had hit him in the throat, cracking the cervical vertebrae.

"Gone wrong," he said, voice expressionless, then fell backward, out of sight, just his boots visible.

There was a second of stillness, broken only by the roaring of the inferno that had virtually destroyed the building behind them.

"Any more?" said Kyle.

"Don't know. Let's go for that jeep."

But it was only a roving patrol, not the major attack that Ted Abbey had been expecting.

Four men in two vehicles. There was a small pickup parked behind the blazing store, its roof showing above a rise in the ground.

Cautiously the three began to walk toward the jeep, guns ready, eyes scanning the empty wilderness that stretched out to the east.

It hadn't occurred to them to question the deaths of the shot men. They'd gone down and lay still, so that was that.

But the first of the attackers, tucked away by Ted Abbey's scattergun, was still alive. His machine pistol lay several yards away from his body, half buried in the sand.

But he rose from the ground, blood leaking from a number of wounds around the top of his right thigh and hip, looming at Carrie Princip like an avenging zombie, mouth open in a soundless scream of hatred.

She was taken by surprise and was knocked to the dirt without a chance to defend herself. Kyle started to turn, way too slow, the rifle dangling uselessly in his hand.

But Sly had been looking toward the jeep. The fire had frightened him, and he didn't want to stare at it any longer. So he saw the man burst into life before any of them.

His initial reaction wasn't quick enough to stop the attack on Carrie, but his mind worked sufficiently fast to swing a clumsy blow with his half-clenched right fist. Sly was very strong. The blow struck the wounded man on the side of the face, near the mouth, cracking his cheekbone and sending him staggering to his knees.

Kyle shot him through the side of the head before he could recover his senses.

CLOSE TO THE FIRE, Sly finished telling the story, convinced deep in his heart that his father heard him.

"So me was a big help, Dad. Carrie and Kyle was real pleased. Now when it's light we all get to got going to find Jim and Heather. She's pretty, Heather. Likes me, as well." He opened his eyes, his communication finished. "There," he said, smiling at the two watchers. "Now me go sleep good."

"Yeah, the sleep of the innocent," said Carrie.

25

The sound drifted out over the snow-covered land.

God rest ye merry, gentlemen,
Let nothing you dismay,
Remember Christ our Savior,
Was born on Christmas Day.
To save us all from Satan's power
When we had gone astray.

The voices of the rest of the survivors of the McGill family joined Mac on the chorus of the old, old song.

"Oh, tidings of comfort and joy, comfort and joy,
Yes, tidings of comfort and joy."

"Bit early for carols, isn't it, Dad?" said Paul, now the oldest of the children.

"Yeah, I guess so. Nearly three weeks, isn't it?"

Mac's first wife, Jeanne, was clutching a pink plastic tumbler of whiskey, reaching up to brush a stray coil of errant brown hair from her dark eyes. "Think we might make it to Muir Woods before the others leave it?"

Angel McGill, hands still showing the pink scars of the bad burns she'd received trying to save the life of her youngest boy, Jack, smiled. "Maybe nobody's there. This snow's probably come down all across California and the West Coast. That's what triggered off the carols and this sudden feeling for Christmas. Like being home in New England, all together."

The Phantasm, the huge RV, occupied most of a turnoff on a narrow side road about sixty miles north of San Francisco. With five adults and two children, the camper was a little crowded.

The other two vehicles were hemmed in by the massive Phantasm, closer to a ring of dead aspens, so that nobody could steal them away in the night. Not that Mac figured there'd be many people around in such snowy and bleak weather.

But they couldn't afford to risk losing the fuel tank, attached to an old jeep. The twelve hundred gallons it had held when they'd fled the far northeast was down to something under four hundred gallons. The third vehicle in their convoy was an elderly European four-by-four that Paul and his dead brother John had worked on for weeks, souping it up until it was capable of nearly one-thirty on a flat highway.

Pamela turned in her seat and pulled back the strip of orange curtain. "Still snowing," she said.

There was a good eighteen inches lying everywhere, and they all knew there weren't going to be any lifesaving plows coming out of the darkness to sweep the way clear for them.

Mac wasn't that worried, though he wished they'd been able to get a little closer to the coast, where the salt air would keep snowfall to a minimum.

He'd found that he was suffering from mood shifts over the past few weeks, something that had never happened before in his life. Since the landing of the *Aquila* and the appalling shock of finding that the United States of America that he'd left was no longer in existence, Mac had realized that he was no longer the man he'd once been.

He never used to doubt himself or find it tough to make decisions in moments of crises. And anyone who suffered from depression had needed, in his simplistic view, a good kick in the ass.

Not now.

Since the space vessel's crash, particularly after he'd completed the odyssey to New England that had resulted in the death of his friend Pete Turner, Mac had become aware that he'd slowed down.

At forty-six he'd been used to working with his brain as a top astrophysicist. And with his body as a relaxation, concentrating on keeping superfit.

After Earthblood it was hard to come to terms with the fact that his mental skills were utterly obsolete and that he had already lost the top edge of his fitness.

And in moments of mortal danger he'd frozen, leaving the saving of his family to his wives and his children.

"Mac." A hand touched his sleeve.

"Sorry," he said, struggling to retrieve a smile for Angel, who was sitting next to him.

"You drifted away from us," she said. "Looked like you'd stared into your own grave."

"Yeah. Something like that. Guess I got a touch of the sads." He shook his head. "Don't worry. Gone now." Looking around at the faces of his wives and his four children, he said, "We got skis with us on the roof here. If it stops snowing tomorrow morning, why don't we go out and get us some pre-Christmas winter sporting?"

The suggestion was greeted with general delight, and Henderson McGill felt much better as he eventually slipped into sleep in his narrow bunk that night.

IT WAS TRULY a heaven of sunrise.

The turnoff overlooked a broad valley, dotted with the blackened corpses of ten thousand trees. But the steady fall of snow had gentled their stark outlines, softening the grim landscape.

It looked as though the vid special-effects men and women had labored to produce an unbelievable view of classical beauty.

Most of the hills were gentle, but a quarter mile to their left there was a much steeper slope, banked with deep, drifted snow, bare rock showing through, glittering with outcrops of quartz.

"Isn't it marvelous, Dad?" said Jocelyn, her small gloved fingers in his.

Yeah, and have you ever thought, honey, that we're all going to die? The words had appeared all unbidden in his brain, but Mac had just enough presence of mind to censor them before they reached his lips.

Instead, he said, "Yeah, and it's all free and ours. No lining up for lifts or equipment hire."

That was much better.

One by one the rest of the family emerged, boots crunching in the frozen, powdery snow, exclaiming at the untouched dome of cloudless blue and the bright sun.

"No chance of hitting the road," said Paul, shaking his head at the blocked highway.

"Not today, son. But there's tomorrow. If Jim and the rest are in Muir Woods, they'll likely wait a couple of days. And they'll manage to leave us a message about where they've gone. Don't worry—" he punched his son lightly on the arm "—not a day for doing any worrying."

Pamela joined them in a quilted suit, her breath frosting the air around her mouth. "Cold as charity," she said. "What're we going to do about guarding the vehicles?"

Mac bit his lip. There it was again. He should have thought of that, not just been ready to go off into the gentle slopes around them for a fun time on skis. Could be any number of thugs and killers around waiting for the chance to get their hands on the vehicles and the gas. And the guns.

And the women.

"Shit, I'll stay and keep watch," he said quickly. "Not that good on skis. Brings out my old knee trouble."

With only mild argument, the rest of the family left Mac to guard the vehicles while they went skiing. There was a good pair of binoculars in the well-equipped Phantasm. Henderson McGill heated himself a mug of chamomile tea and sat in the driver's seat, watching through the glasses.

Even at seven, little Jocelyn was already showing signs of becoming an excellent skier, cutting her way down the gentle incline to the right of the blocked road. The rest of the family were all with her, etching patterns in the virgin snow. Mac wound down the driver's window, smiling at the echoing laughter that came rippling toward him.

There was no sign of any other human life.

Once he spotted a pair of elks, picking their delicate way through the deep carpet of white, a mile or more away across the valley. Not long after that, he was raking the skyline with the binoculars and saw what he figured was a small pack of hunting wolves, moving fast on the trail of the elk.

Far, far away, to the north and east, Mac thought he could pick up a faint smudge of what might have been smoke rising vertically into the calm morning sky.

It was becoming warmer, and he could see a tiny thread of water inching along the side of the highway where the snow was beginning to thaw. If that kept up throughout the rest of the day, it might mean a chance of their getting moving again within forty-eight hours or so.

Angel attracted his attention, waving her arms, the silvered ski poles shimmering in the bright sunlight.

"Hey, dumb ass!"

"What?"

"Want me to spell you on watch?"

Mac shook his head. "No. Thanks, lover, but I don't mind. I'll heat up some soup in a half hour or so."

She was less than a hundred yards away from him, her blond hair tangled by her exertion. Her cheeks were flushed, and Mac thought how beautiful she looked. And remembered again why he'd married her.

"You enjoying it?" he shouted.

"Too easy. You see Sukie giving it a good shot? Hope this Aurora turns out to be somewhere with some decent snow in winter. That'd be real good."

"Who knows?" he responded, shrugging his shoulders. For a moment it crossed his mind to ask her to slip back into the RV with him just for a little while. The idea of hugging and cuddling Angel seemed a real good one, but the kids would be back soon and he hated being interrupted in lovemaking.

"I'm going there!" she yelled, pointing to the left and the steep, craggy slope.

Mac nodded, half his mind still on the idea of getting Angel into bed with him. "Sure," he said, mostly to himself. "But you take care."

She shook her head, pointing to her muffled ears. "Can't hear you, love."

"Said to take care," he called out, louder this time.

Angel waved and set off across the face of the gentle hillside, working her way with effortless skill toward the top of the farther, angled slope.

Mac stood and reached for a catering-size can of soup from one of the capacious storage closets on the RV. He glanced through the ingredients, noting the amazing range of additives and coloring agents and flavoring agents and preserving agents that the soup contained.

With the effects of Earthblood still leaching their way through the planet's ecostructure, he guessed that it would be a long, long while before any fresh canned food became available. If ever. And when it did, there wasn't likely to be a string of coded letters and numbers packed into it.

The way that green shoots were grudgingly beginning to appear here and there through the dried crimson blight made it seem a possibility that one day the tiny number of survivors might be able to eat fresh fruit and vegetables again.

"One day," he said, putting the glutinous contents of the can into the large enameled pan and placing it carefully onto low heat.

There was a flurry of fresh snow when he looked out of the window, but the trickle of water was wider and the temperature was obviously still rising.

There was a snowball fight going on between his children, with Jeanne favoring the two young girls against Paul and Pamela. Mac took up the binoculars once more and adjusted the focus with the milled black plastic wheel, bringing the faraway contest into sharp detail.

Jocelyn was laughing her head off, mouth open wide with delight, the distance turning the fight into a mime. She had just hit Paul flush in the face with a handful of packed snow, making him look like an enraged Santa Claus.

That thought made Henderson McGill wonder again about the rapid approach of Christmas.

The last family ceremony had been Pamela's birthday on November 18. The warm, caring ritual full of happiness and emotion that in an instant had turned the white Victorian house up on Melville Avenue to a charnel house of death and bare-bones violence.

Mac shook his head and laid down the glasses, getting up to check the soup. It was just beginning to bubble gently around the edges. He took a ladle out of the cutlery drawer and stirred it for a few moments, worried about the chance of it sticking. There was a row of spice jars in a neat rosewood rack, and he added a few pinches of turmeric and some cumin to give the bland soup some extra flavoring.

He tasted it. "Not bad. Maybe I'll take up cooking for real when we get to Aurora," he said.

A noise outside made him start. Quickly he wiped condensation from the window and peered into the bright sunlight. The sound was repeated, but this time he saw what was happening. The warmth of the day was melting the snow, sending it tumbling off the low branches of the dead trees in great wet clumps.

"Could be on the move in a day or so," he said, then tutted at the realization that he seemed to be talking to himself a lot recently, wondering if this was the male menopause that he'd read about in a magazine only a couple of days before blasting off into space in the *Aquila*.

Another bunch of snow fell heavily, landing on the domed top of the fuel tank with a hollow ringing noise. The melt was gathering momentum.

A sudden thought struck Mac, and he looked around for the binoculars. "Place is turning into a dump," he muttered.

Finally he spotted it on the bench seat, half-hidden by Sukie's favorite doll, a droopy trollop that rejoiced in the name of Mournful Megg. He took up the glasses and went to the window that gave the best view of the steep, overhung cliff where Angel had said she was going to ski.

Now he was aware of the melodious tinkling of water, running musically off the roof of the RV, down onto the rutted ice of the highway.

The glass was steamed up from the simmering pan of soup, and again he wiped it with a shirt-sleeve, finding that his fingers were trembling when he lifted the binoculars. The lenses were clouded with condensation.

"There," he breathed, finally aiming them toward where he'd last seen her, twisting the control until he located the twin trails of her skis vanishing among the trees, heading upward.

He found them again, higher, much higher.

He scanned the slope until he finally picked up a darting, twisting figure, cutting her own piste with a skillful agility that took his breath.

Mac watched Angel, his peripheral vision picking up the monstrous slab of undercut snow that toppled soundlessly above her. Frozen in disbelief, he saw it race down in a surging cloud of immense destruction, snapping off trees like matchwood.

Overwhelming and burying her.

26

The chief of the Hunters of the Sun sat waiting patiently in her office, contentedly turning the thin pages of the old nineteenth-century novel. *Pride and Prejudice* was one of her true all-time favorites.

It was a book that she always enjoyed reading just before going into an interrogation, particularly if it promised to be something a little special.

And Jeff Thomas, ex-journalist, accomplished liar and one-time crew member of the USSV *Aquila,* looked as though he might be real interesting.

The name of the chief, though hardly any of the subordinates knew it, was Margaret Tabor. She was twenty-seven years old and had been the mistress and associate of the man called Flagg. Not even she knew what his real name had been.

But she knew how important names were. Her degree in socio-psychology at UCLA had brought her few friends, but it had brought one young man, named Owen Johnson, who had discovered while hacking into the college's personal files that she had a middle name. One that came from way back on her mother's side. Dildow. Owen had told this fascinating bit of information to four of his close companions, and they'd begun to make her life intolerable with their sneers and scurrilous jokes.

By an extraordinary coincidence all five young men died in bizarre accidents within eleven days of each other. And their sneering died with them. The middle name of Margaret Tabor also vanished forever, disappearing from all of the computer files overnight.

Flagg had contacts at some colleges, and when he came to hear about the strange deaths, he made some connections. That led to a meeting and then to a strangely conventional sexual liaison between himself and the younger woman.

Now Flagg was dead . . . and she had work to do.

By now her assistant should be over in the farthest wing of the large quasimilitary complex that held Jeff Thomas, along with several other itinerant prisoners. Soon she would be talking to him about Aurora.

And other things.

JOE ENJOYED HIS WORK.

Before Earthblood he'd been happy in a slaughterhouse in Bowling Green, Kentucky. Death fascinated him, and the power of inflicting it gave him a profoundly sexual pleasure. But stupid sheep and cows and spavined mares had gotten to be boring.

Now, once he'd been enlisted into the Hunters of the Sun, Joe was dealing with people. Admittedly most of them were half-starved crips, but it was still better.

There was something about this one—Veronica Poole was the name chalked on the board outside her cell—that was sort of special. Admittedly she was gut-churningly antique and wrinkled, but her body was like that of a woman twenty years younger. The idea of having a little sport with Ms. Poole before letting her dangle off the hook had been a bright one.

And she sure was eager, thought Joe, grinning to himself. Very eager, since she thought that it just might save her miserable old life.

Now she was kneeling in front of him, hands reaching imploringly for him. The marks of his fingers were bright across her cheek. The guard's eye was caught by a flicker of movement across the corridor. That limp-dick little bastard, trying to peek out through the grille on his door.

"Move the hell away, Thomas!" he shouted, making the cringing woman start in surprise. "You don't get off watching me getting blown."

Now she was touching him, rubbing him gently. Joe put one hamlike hand on the back of her skull and roughly jerked her closer.

He laughed again, feeling the tension already rising in expectation of a surging orgasm.

But instead of the beginnings of pleasure he was hit by pain so appalling that his mind simply refused to admit it.

Joe's eyes closed and his mouth jerked open, blood worming out from where he'd just bitten the end clear off his tongue. His arms spread wide as if he'd been suddenly crucified. But he didn't make a sound, couldn't make a sound.

His entire body was paralyzed by the violence of the white agony centered at his groin.

Nanci was up off her knees, her lips peeled back from her teeth in a terrifying rictus of hatred. Her right hand was clamped around the guard's testicles, nails digging in with appalling ferocity, twisting the scrotal sac, grinding it up against the sharp point of the pubic bone.

Her left hand reached up toward Joe's shuttered eyes.

He felt no more pain, his brain already overloaded, but a tiny part of his mind was aware of a jagged intrusion beneath his eyelids. Probing and tearing. Warm liquid soaked his cheeks, and an infinite blackness was hovering about him.

Then he seemed to be floating. For a moment he thought of something really important that he wanted to say, but the words slithered away from him like a hand filled to overflowing with buttery maggots.

The floating stopped…and his breathing stopped.

The pain in his lower abdomen seemed to have eased, but now there was a terrible cutting agony in his throat. He struggled to draw breath, but his mouth was filled with the hot iron taste of blood.

Nanci took the Port Royale from his shoulder, one of her Heckler & Koch handguns from his belt. She moved away as the dying man's heels began to drum against the wall in the neural spasm that preceded his slow passing from life.

In his cell Jeff heard the sound of a scuffle, but he didn't dare to go again and peer through the narrow slit in his door. He sat on his bunk, head in his hands, mind racing over what was going to happen to him. He tried to concentrate on the lies he'd already told his inquisitors and the new ones that he might soon have to come up with.

He was aware of the smell of excrement drifting in, but he ignored it. Jeff had been in that part of the prison complex long enough to be used to it. Most of the victims of the wire-and-hook technique fouled themselves in their lingering agony.

Nanci was standing still, waiting and listening.

A doctor would have found that her pulse and respiration were only fractionally above normal.

"Thomas," she breathed. If it really was the long-lost Jeff Thomas in that room across the passage, then it might be a delightful and unexpected bonus. It would be nice to see good old Jeff again, remind him how he'd walked away and left her to die out in the desert.

Her grip tightened for a moment on the butt of the 15-round automatic.

Behind her Ed unlocked the door and walked through, hopeful of getting himself a piece of the action before the woman got strung up on the wall.

He found himself looking straight down the railroad-tunnel muzzle of a big handgun.

"Close the door," she whispered so that the tall guard could barely hear her. "Slow and easy. Or I spill your guts on the floor. Now."

Ed was staring at the blood-drenched corpse of his friend, face swollen and disfigured as he hung from the hook. The smell of excrement and death filled the corridor.

"You . . . how d'you . . . who helped you?"

"Nobody." She stepped close to him. "Close the door, slow and easy now." She was watching him, listening to hear the lock click shut. "Good. You're going to get to live awhile. That other door leads to the outside, does it?"

"Yeah, it do."

"Excellent. You may go to the top of the class. One more question. Where is the motor pool?"

"I'm sorry," he said, concentrating on squeezing his buttocks together to stop losing control. "Don't know what..."

"Where are the vehicles kept? I believe that it might be in a compound just beyond this outer door. We came in that way, unless my sense of direction had departed from me. So, am I correct in locating the trucks and cars?"

"Why, yes, ma'am." He was sweating so much it was running in his eyes, but the man didn't dare even blink. Never in his life had anything terrified him as much as this sixty-year-old teacher lady.

"The bolts do the door?"

"Sure do. Chief don't like too many keys. Cells and all bolt on the outside. That one on the inside. Door behind me needs a key to get in."

Nanci smiled at him. "That is wonderful. You can be the blackboard monitor for all of next week."

"Thank you, lady." He was so relieved that she didn't appear to be angry with him that he wasn't even listening to what the woman was actually saying to him.

"Lie down."

"Sorry?"

She pointed with the muzzle of the gun. "On the floor, on your stomach."

"Why?" He looked puzzled.

"Because my friends Mr. Koch and Mr. Heckler here say so."

The man got to his hands and knees, looking up at Nanci to make sure he was doing good. He really wanted to do good. When she nodded approvingly at him, the man lay right down, rolling onto his belly, resting the side of his cheek against the rough concrete floor, trying not to weep with fear.

Jeff Thomas was also becoming scared. The woman should have been dead by now. But he'd heard the other guard, the nicer one, Ed, come into the passage. Then there'd been some talk, so quiet he couldn't catch what was being said.

"Hey, out there," he called very quietly, his curiosity overcoming his fear.

Nobody answered, so he stayed where he was, sitting on his small bed.

Ed blinked open his eyes, seeing from his lowly position that the teacher lady was real close. One polished boot was on either side of his head, heels touching his neck. Then weight on his shoulders as she lowered herself onto his back.

It wasn't an unpleasant feeling. In fact, it produced a tiny frisson of excitement riding through his terror.

"Hands gripping the nice ironed seams of your pants, son, if you please."

"Yes, ma'am."

There was the breath of steel on leather as she holstered the powerful 9 mm pistol. Nanci braced herself, setting her feet firmly astride the guard's shaved skull. Leaning forward, she quickly clasped her hands under his chin, aware of the slight stubble against her palms.

Jeff heard the odd noise.

If he'd been an outdoor type, he might have compared it to the snapping of a dry branch.

But he wasn't. City born and bred. So it reminded him of a powerful security bolt snapping shut.

Nanci sat back, waiting for the last twitches and jerks to cease. A dark pool of urine was spreading across the floor from between the thighs of the corpse. Finally only the index finger on the man's left hand still moved, the nail scratching backward and forward for several seconds.

She sighed, closing her eyes for a moment.

There was a light rapping on the door at her back, accompanied by a muffled voice.

"Time to go, Nanci," she said, straightening herself up from her seat on the dead man's shoulders.

"Hey, you guys! Ed! Joe! Come on, guys. Chief wants the prisoner, Thomas."

She heard movement from within the cell. Someone standing up and shuffling feet.

"Chief'll get pissed! Pissed at me an' you two. Just hook the old slut and open up."

Nanci considered opening the door and letting in whoever was out there. But she was already ahead of the game. Two guards. Two corpses. Eventually, if she waited for too long, the odds would stack against her and the game would end.

Then the prisoner in the cell put in his two bits. "Hey, whoever's there. Better let him in. He's the chief's lieutenant. I know his voice. You'll just likely get us both into deep shit!" Jeff's voice was high and ragged, making Nanci smile.

She walked toward the cell door, heels clicking, one hand on the butt of the Heckler & Koch, the machine pistol slung over her shoulders. She reached out to slide the bolt open.

"Hello, Jeff. What a pleasant surprise to meet up with you again."

27

The chief wasn't very happy.

Her assistant had called through from the isolated cell block to report that he hadn't been able to get any response from the two guards. As a consequence, he wasn't able to bring the prisoner, Jeff Thomas, along to her rooms at the scheduled time. But they were going to find the second set of keys as soon as possible and get inside. He'd report when he could.

Margaret Tabor had placed the telephone back very gently onto its rest. She put the tips of her fingers together like a child playing "church and steeple."

"Yes," she said to her empty office.

It was no surprise to her when the news came through only seconds later that a four-by-four pickup had burst through the main gate, leaving a number of blazing vehicles behind it, cutting their transportation capability by two-thirds.

When her skinny assistant eventually appeared at her door, looking as if he'd just developed an ulcer, she had even managed a thin-lipped smile designed to reassure him. It scared him even more.

"Not your fault," she said. "But it's someone's fault, isn't it?"

"Sure is, Chief," he admitted, eager to deflect the blame, his fingers playing nervously with the badge on his lapel.

"Whose?"

He had survived relatively unscarred the last few months of Flagg's rule, and had already learned the different ways of Margaret Tabor. She didn't mind honest admissions of failure, but it was better not to try to wriggle your way out of trouble by deceit or by lying to her.

"Can't have been Thomas. Someone opened his cell after they butchered the guards."

He laid some instant pix of the scene on her desk, one by one, as though playing some macabre game of patience. She leaned forward and scanned them, face showing no emotion.

"Something is very wrong here," she said.

"No evidence of anyone else being involved. Just this . . ." He consulted a small notepad. "Veronica Poole. Teacher aged about sixty. From Fort Worth. The guard, Joe, was supposed to be hooking her. Doesn't figure."

"Woman of sixty, alone and unarmed, did this. . . ." She waved her hand at the livid photographs. "Got a big man up on her own. Gouged out his eyes. She somehow overcame him. Got his gun . . . what was he carrying?"

He rifled the pages. "Oh, yeah. Something else odd. The old woman had a Port Royale machine pistol. Sixteen round, like an Uzi. Joe had it. Seems he also took one of a pair of matching Heckler & Koch P-111s that she'd been carrying. Nine-millimeter automatics. Fifteen round. Other guard had a standard .38."

"Wait, wait. This old woman had weapons of that quality on her and nobody told me about it?"

"I didn't know, Chief."

Margaret Tabor nodded slowly. She reached for a yellow pad and then stopped. "Who interrogated her?"

"Miller and McCabe. I checked."

"And neither of them thought that it was odd to find... Let it pass. This is spilled milk. Bring me the folder on Mistress Poole and the black file on people we're supposed to be looking out for. Right away."

MCCABE SAT on the floor, holding a kerchief to his broken nose, trying not to bleed on the carpet of her office. He was white as parchment, hands trembling.

"This is something very serious. And you missed it."

"I'm sorry, Chief," he mumbled through the blood and splintered teeth.

"No," Margaret Tabor said very quietly. "Mistake like that doesn't get you sorry, McCabe. It gets you dead."

AFTER THE MAN had been taken away to the narrow passage with the rusting iron hooks in its wall, Margaret Tabor sat and looked at the slim file on Nanci Simms.

The light blue eyes stared back at her from a slightly blurred snatched photograph. It was a street in small-town America, and the woman was glancing sideways, as though she'd somehow detected the click of a hidden camera. From the car that appeared in the picture, it looked as if it had been taken several years ago, around the mid 2030s.

There was surprisingly little information on her. No birth date, no birthplace. Nothing on parents. No home. No friends. No social security number or bank details, though it did mention her most common pseudonym of Veronica Poole and the phony job record of English literature teacher in Fort Worth.

Height of five feet eleven was followed by a question mark, showing it was only a guess. Same with the weight and age. Approximately sixty years old, it said.

The rest was a jumbled mass of supposition and partial information. What came through was a dangerous woman who'd been around a lot. Traveled in Europe and extensively in the Far and Middle East. Was believed to have flourished as an undercover assassin for several years. Skilled in armed- and unarmed-combat techniques.

"You got that bit right," said the chief, laying the folder back down.

Someone who might have worked for Zelig... who might well have known where the opposition headquarters of Aurora was hidden.

It was bitterly frustrating to have had this lethal woman safe and snug in a cell. A chicken ready for the plucking. And then to lose her...

The chief of the Hunters of the Sun glanced at her wrist chron. Just forty-five minutes had passed since Nanci Simms had butchered two experienced guards and broken out of the compound with an important prisoner. She wouldn't have gotten too far away in less than an hour.

The red button on her desk intercom brought an instant response from her assistant. "Yes, Chief?"

"Get the chopper out."

"Now?"

"No. I thought around about the end of February would be a real good time."

"Sorry, Chief."

"Being sorry doesn't butter the turnips, does it?"

"No."

"I want a search for that woman. We know what she's driving. Probably she'll have headed north. Toward where we think... Then again, she might try and second- or third-guess us. Tell the pilot to sector the land for... for fifty miles around."

"That takes us to the hills."

"Yes."

"We don't have too much gas for the chopper at this particular temporal window, Chief. Difficult to get our hands on more of it right now."

"We'll manage."

"Sure, Chief."

IT WASN'T too much of a surprise to Margaret Tabor when the helicopter pilot reported back to her two hours later. "Fuel arrow was down in the red, Chief."

"So I would expect. And you found nothing."

It was a plain, calm statement, not a question. But the woman pilot chose to treat it as a question. "Nothing. Spotlight picked up tracks, heading off into the back country. Toward the north. Then they went onto a ribbon of old blacktop, and that was where I lost it. Quartered the whole area. Long as I could.''

"Don't feel bad about it. Looks like we thought we had us an old, harmless sheep in our trap. Turned out we caught a real vicious wolverine.''

28

It was Jeanne who finally managed to persuade Henderson McGill to stop the hopeless task of trying to retrieve the buried corpse of Angel McGill.

The others had all tried.

After the thunderous avalanche had swept half a mountain of thawing snow down the steep cliff, erasing the woman from life in a handful of seconds, the whole family had rushed to the scene. Paul had been there first, skiing from the other side of the broad valley, slicing across with speed and control, glancing up above him to see whether there was any danger of a further fall. But the rock face had been scoured clear.

By the time Mac himself had strapped on a pair of skis from the back of the Phantasm and lumbered clumsily to join the others, there was only silence. The spray and turbulence of the avalanche was over. Already there were dozens of birds appearing, eager to find whether any potential food might have been revealed from beneath the snow cover.

Mac had slung a shovel across his shoulders as he left the huge RV. While the others looked unbelievingly at the massive fall, he had started digging, working like a demented fury, clawing his way into the mixture of snow and water and mud.

"No point, Dad," said Paul. "We don't even know where she might be." The mountainous pile was fully three hundred yards long and at least forty feet high.

"There's a chance," Mac had panted.

But there had never been any sort of a chance.

It took Jeanne's hand on his arm to persuade Mac to finally give up the pointless, hopeless struggle. His own hands were blistered and raw, his back a tangle of strained muscle.

"Come in, love," said Jeanne gently.

"She's gone." He straightened painfully, dropping the scratched shovel at his feet. "By God, but she's gone. Just plucked away from us. No goodbyes."

"It's often the way." Jeanne looked around. "Thaw's still going on."

"Yeah. I guess we... Oh, Christ!" His hands covered his face, shoulders heaving. Jeanne put her arms tightly around him and held him like a child while the sorrow shook him. She hugged him and whispered her love.

Eventually Mac sighed, swallowing hard and trying for a smile. "All right, now," he said softly. "I can deal with it. But there's so much damnable death around. Seems that where I let my shadow fall, somebody goes to meet their Maker. It's not rightly fair, Jeanne."

"We have to keep moving, love."

"I know it. But there were ten of us only a few weeks ago. Ten of us, all close and loving."

"We're still close and loving, Mac."

"Less than three weeks. And three of our little ones dead. Now Angel torn away."

"Come inside and rest. Way the snow's going we could maybe try to move on in another day."

Mac blew his nose. "Life's turned upside down for us. Nothing makes sense, you know."

But he allowed her to lead him back to the RV, where the four surviving children were waiting for them.

ALTHOUGH THEY DIDN'T even know where Angel's mangled body was buried, early the next morning they held a kind of a service for her. One by one they said a few words about how they remembered her. The good times. The laughter.

Even Sukie, four years old, managed to overcome her sorrow to say farewell to her mother.

Afterward they all hugged, together in a tight circle of grief.

The following morning Mac rose early and stood outside in the pallid glow of the false dawn, looking across the monstrous pile of snow and earth along the valley.

The narrow stream, frozen over when they'd become trapped by the blizzard, was now swollen into a frothing brown torrent. Patches of the highway showed in spots through the melting snow, and it looked as if they could get moving again.

Mac had slept badly. He'd gone through periods of restless turning, eyes open, listening to the steady, sullen drip of water all around the vehicle. The thought of the deaths of the loved members of his family lay more heavily on his mind. Even when he slithered into brief moments of sleep, his mind's eye was flooded with terrible images of his children and his young wife suffering ghastly deaths while he stood by, unable to do anything to help them.

Before opening the door and going out into the morning, Mac had taken down his shotgun, the blued-steel imported Brazzi 16-gauge weapon, holding five rounds. The stock was cold and damp to the touch.

His breath feathered out around him as he looked at the dark, blighted landscape, clouds gathering toward the west where Jim Hilton and the others might be waiting for them. Mac imagined that he could taste salt, carried on the breeze from the Pacific Ocean.

The gun felt heavy in his hands, and he stared down at it, his mind blanking, unable to remember why he'd brought it out with him. Mac watched as his right thumb eased off the safety and his index finger moved to the trigger.

His brow furrowed, wondering where the enemy was. His gun was ready for an enemy.

"The last enemy is death," he whispered, without any idea where the words had come from.

The muzzle of the scattergun was huge, seeming to suck him down into it.

"No more pain," he said.

The door of the vehicle opened behind him, but Henderson McGill was locked too deep into his own bleak sadness to be aware of it.

"Hi, Dad."

"What?" He responded from somewhere far away, louder than he'd intended, making his youngest child, Sukie, jump and nearly slip off the top step. She was wearing a blue dressing gown, her eyes still heavy with sleep.

"What're you doing, Dad?" she asked, vaguely curious at the sight of her father cradling the glittering weapon in his lap, the stock between his knees, the end of the barrel pointing toward his face. His finger was white on the trigger.

"Doing, honey?" He felt like a man trapped on the sticky border between waking and darkness.

"That's real dangerous, Dad." She moved to stand on the same step where he was sitting and touched the Brazzi. "Never point a gun unless you're going to use it."

Mac nodded, eyes misting with tears. Suddenly he was aware of the lonely road that he'd been about to walk, shocked at the realization that if his little girl had woken a couple of minutes later she'd have walked out to find herself covered in blood and brains and splintered bones.

"That's true, honey. Wasn't thinking straight."

"Thinking in bendy lines, were you?"

He hugged her, feeling her frail body. "Yeah. I was thinking in seriously bendy lines, honey."

She looked around in the growing light. "Snow's gone real fast, Daddy."

"And we'll soon be going real fast, as well. To join up with Uncle Jim and the others." He stood up, the gun dangling in his hand like a forgotten gift. "But first we'll start up some coffee and breakfast and wake the others. What d'you say to that, honey? Sound good to you?"

She nodded and kissed him on his cold cheek.

JIM HILTON WAS STIRRING the oatmeal in the kettle, squatted down on his haunches.

The weather had changed in the past forty-eight hours as the wind veered around, bringing warmth and chasing the snow away from Muir Woods.

"What day is it, Dad?"

Heather was standing by the truck, rubbing her hands together, her steady blue-gray eyes taking in the morning.

"Eighth of December."

"You said we'd wait until the eighth."

He nodded. "Right. Looks like it's just you and me heading north toward Aurora."

"Will there be other children there?"

"Don't know." He added hastily, "But I'm certain that there will be."

"Girls my age?"

"Of course. And boys."

Heather sniffed. "Bad news, Dad. Boys are just gross gherkins, and all they want is to get in your pants."

Jim Hilton stopped stirring and looked up at his daughter, startled. "How's that?"

"Andrea had a friend. Kyrie Ellison. Her mom was big in promo-vids. She told us that."

It crossed his mind that this might be a good moment to embark on a serious father-to-daughter conversation on the subject of personal relationships but decided almost immediately that it would involve opening a can of worms he'd much rather leave firmly closed.

"Breakfast's nearly ready," he said.

"We going, then?"

"I suppose so."

"Leave a message?"

"Course."

"Do you think that the others...?" The sentence faded away into the dank, dripping stillness.

Jim sighed. "I'll sort of be surprised if I don't ever meet up again with old Mac this side of the Pearly Gates. Tough son of a space suit, Mac. Kyle and Steve and Carrie and the rest... I just can't even begin to make a guess. The world's turned upside down, Heather."

"I bet that Nanci makes it."

Jim didn't particularly want to pursue that line of conversation, either, and he busied himself with dishing out the steaming oatmeal.

"Maybe," he said. "Eat this before it gets cold. We'll have a last look around and then leave before noon."

"Can I go to the gift shop again, Dad?"

"No. Yeah. Not if you bring any more surplus junk along with you."

"Junk!" Her voice for a moment reminded him with agonizing clarity of his dead sweetheart from high school days, Lori. "What junk?"

"Wind chimes made from hand-colored mica. Place mats showing the Golden Gate Bridge. That doll that you filled with gunk and then squeezed it and..."

"It did the business," she said, squeaking with delight. "You laughed, Dad, at that."

"Laughing to keep from puking, Heather. And those slices of wood."

"Burls. They grew, didn't they? No Earthblood on them."

It was true. Heather had found the wrecked gift shop and eatery, with everything edible or drinkable gone. But the shelves of souvenirs of Muir Woods remained, including the redwood burls and hundreds of packets of seeds of all sorts. The girl had spent hours out on her own in the cold and wet, cultivating a small patch of ground and planting all of the seeds. Wildflowers and shrubs and squashes. Jim reckoned that most of them would die, but some might make it.

A small start to the greening of the ailing planet.

"And no more piñon candles, Heather."

"All right, Dad, but... What's that?"

Jim had already heard the sound, a crackling in the brush, not too far away on the other side of their van. He drew the Ruger Blackhawk Hunter in what had become an easy reflex action in the past three months and put his finger to his lips.

"Animal," mouthed the girl, catching the hoarse, snuffling noise.

He stood up, waiting.

Something was padding through the wet mud and leaf mold that lay everywhere.

He had spotted tracks all around their camp every morning. Some of them looked like the marks of a sizable bear, but he'd never been that good on identifying spoor when he'd been doing his survivalist courses.

"Dad."

It was a bear.

Black bear.

Jim eased the hammer down on the powerful handgun, smiling at the fat little cub as it rolled its way past the dented front of their trusty van. It couldn't have been more than a couple of months old, its bright button eyes staring fearlessly up at the two intruders.

"Cute," said Jim.

"Shoot it, quick, Dad. Be good eating."

"It's a little cub." He was shocked at his daughter's instant, cold-blooded reaction. "I couldn't... Heather, it'd be like blasting Bambi."

"Bullshit, Dad." Her hand reached for the Ruger. "Give it me, if you won't do it. We *need* meat."

It was true.

The kick of the gun ran to his shoulder, and the furry bundle rolled over dead. The echoes of the shot seemed to ring through the trees forever.

As father and daughter began together to butcher the little carcass, Jim kept his handgun ready. He knew from books and vids that the next likely event would be the appearance of the giant, enraged mother of the cub.

But nothing happened.

The melting snow continued to drip from the trees, and low clouds blew their sullen way across the forest. The blood ran away, turning pink in the trickling water, and Jim tossed the furry skin and innards off into the undergrowth.

A profound depression settled over his soul.

The memories of so many deaths plagued him, and he began to anticipate a future that seemed ever more hopeless. Despite the occasional clues, there was no real guarantee that Aurora even existed.

Perhaps they'd never find it and wander the deserted blacktops and avoid the hostile fortress communities forever, just he and Heather. Until death would relieve them of their lonely suffering.

He stood up and wiped the blade of his sheath knife in the soft earth, then dried it on the leg of his pants. Being on the move again would be the only way of shaking off the pervading sadness, he decided.

"We going, Dad?"

"Yeah. I'll find a good place to leave a note for the others. If they are . . . I'll nail it up to the board by the main entrance to the woods."

Just then they both spun around, alerted by the sudden noise. Out of the shadows beneath the trees something big and bulky was rushing fast toward them. Breathing harsh and heavy.

Jim drew the Ruger and waited, motioning Heather to stand behind him.

The large shape burst out, water glistening on its shoulders, teeth bared.

Bared in a smile.

"Hi Jim and hi Heather. It me, Sly."

29

Jeff Thomas couldn't stand the suspense.

When he'd heard the voice of Nanci Simms as she threw back the bolts on his cell door, the ex-journalist of the *West American* had nearly fainted. It wasn't something that he'd ever done before, though there'd been some desperate moments during his twenty-five years of life.

He'd stood up slowly, but the small room seemed to have filled with a dense mist. His own voice sounded hollow and very far away. "Hi, Nanci. What a surprise."

"We're leaving, Jeff. Now."

She took his arm as he stumbled and nearly fell. Then she thrust a heavy .38 in his belt. "Pull yourself together. Flake out on me now, Jefferson, and I'll cause you some swift and grievous suffering before I kill you."

"I didn't mean to leave you," he heard himself mumbling as they moved out into the corridor. "How's your leg?" But it seemed as if the woman wasn't hearing him. He felt as if he wanted to throw up on the floor.

When he saw the two examples of Nanci's brutal handiwork, he did throw up.

"We'll talk about you leaving me in a while. First things first, Jefferson."

He remembered her sliding back the massive security bolts on the door at the end of the corridor. The surge of cool fresh air, cleansed the stench of blood and death for a few precious moments.

Then they were in a surprisingly clean four-by-four and hurtling through darkness, breaking a fence and shots whizzing around them.

But it was all like a dream.

Nanci was at his side, lips tight, whistling "Marching through Georgia" quietly to herself as she steered the vehicle over sand and rock. She was driving much faster than Jeff thought wise—not that he was going to tell her.

He wasn't about to say anything.

Nanci broke the silence when they'd been going for something close to forty-five minutes.

"She'll put a chopper up after us."

"Who?"

"Woman they call the chief of the Hunters of the Sun. Learned her name. Margaret Tabor. Used to be Flagg's mistress. It's possible she chilled him and made it look like food poisoning. Guess that we shall never know the truth about that.''

''Why would she bother to send a helicopter after us? Two guards can't matter that much.''

''Your brain would make a rabbit's turd look like a bowling ball, Jefferson.''

''Well,'' he said in a pained voice, but decided now wasn't a time to take insult.

''Nothing to do with guards. What you have to realize is that this country now lies between two causes. Between anarchy and freedom. Light and dark. Yin and yang. Call it what you like, and you still got Zelig and all of those backing the ideal of Aurora—the dawn, Jefferson. Set against the militaristic dictatorship of the Hunters of the Sun.''

''But you don't know where that is, do you? Aurora? I don't.''

''They don't know that we don't know. They screwed up in a big way, Jefferson. Took too long to interrogate you properly... and didn't recognize who I was. We were lucky. By now she'll have realized who they let slip. They want us back so they'll try hard. That's why we're going to ground as soon as I can locate a suitable place to hide from air recon.''

Jeff grinned. He was beginning to think that Nanci was going to forgive him for his minor mistake of leaving her to die from a severed artery, alone in the desert.

Nanci rolled the vehicle to a halt, spotting some abandoned outbuildings beyond a dried creek. "Been over some bare rocks, so they should lose the trail. She won't know which way we've gone. And I wonder if I can outguess her. I can." Switching off the engine, she smiled at her companion. "We have at least four or five hours before it'll be safe to move on. Plenty of time for a little lesson on manners, Jefferson."

"No, please, Nanci."

"Oh, yes, dear boy. This is going to please Nanci a great deal. I can promise you that."

THE MCGILL CONVOY picked its slow and careful way westward across what had once been the wealthiest state, finding a way via blue highways and dirt roads toward San Francisco then north into Muir Woods. They'd be late on the agreed date, but by no more than four or five days.

Muir Woods, where some or all of the others might be waiting for them...or maybe none of them, depending on what luck, skill or blind fate dealt them.

Mac plotted his route each day with Jeanne, Paul and Pamela, trying to watch out for any communities where confrontational danger might lie and keeping clear of the high ground, where the snow might still be a problem.

He drove the RV, with Sukie and Jocelyn playing contentedly in the back. Paul was in charge of the jeep that towed their shrinking supply of fuel, while Pamela and Jeanne took turns at the wheel of the souped-up four-by-four, bringing up the rear of their convoy.

They hardly saw anyone.

Once they came across a roadblock built from a tangle of rotten branches. It was in a narrow valley, with no way to get past on either side. Mac stopped a hundred yards away from it, peering cautiously out to see if this could be an ambush. But there was no sign of life.

"Cover me," he called, climbing down from the cab, the SIG-Sauer P-230 in his hand, one of the pump-action Winchesters slung across his shoulder. Somehow he'd turned against his own Brazzi scattergun in the past day or so.

There was a stillness to the afternoon.

The pewter clouds had drifted away, leaving patches of high cumulus dappling a pale blue sky. The temperature had begun to fall again, and he was worried that more snow might intervene before they covered the last miles to Muir Woods.

There was a hand-painted notice propped at the corner of the roadblock. The kind that had become only too familiar since the *Aquila*'s return to Earth.

Aquarius Welcomes No One. Turn Back. No Gas No Food No Water No Beds No Room.

"Thanks a lot," said Mac, walking carefully closer. "Welcome to Aquarius, the xenophobia capital of California."

There wasn't anyone guarding the twenty-foot-high mass of jagged, broken wood.

At least, nobody living.

Mac's guess was that the man, if it had been male, had died at least three weeks ago. The clothes were wind-washed rags, the skin tight and leathery, tanned almost black. As usual, all the soft tissue of the body had long gone. Eyes, lips, face. And some creature had worried at the torso, tearing away the flesh. There was a small-caliber single-shot rifle across what had once been the sentry's lap.

Paul walked up to join Mac at his signal that there was no danger.

"Where's this Aquarius place?" he asked, glancing at the high sides of the cliffs looming above them.

Mac holstered the handgun. "Could be anywhere around. He's been dead for a while. They never came to move him or sent a replacement.

Chances are the settlement's inhabitants died of illness or . . . or something.''

"Can't get around it," said Paul McGill, running his fingers through his luxuriant beard. "Burn it?"

His father considered that option. "Suppose that's best. Bring up a couple of gallons of gas. It might draw attention to us, though."

Paul nodded. "Sure. But I don't figure that'll be a problem. Set the fire, then get ready to roll. This stuff should burn easily, Dad."

"Then we'll do it."

The blaze was ferociously fierce, the flames raging nearly a hundred feet high, the radiant heat making Mac shield his face from over by their vehicles. His son had been right. Within less than ten minutes the block had burned down enough for them to take a run at it, but they waited until there were no signs of live embers to continue on.

There had been no shots, and nobody came after them as they drove out and along the winding road toward the west and the cold, dark sea. There were some torn tents and a couple of tumbledown shacks by a stagnant pool, which might have been all that remained of the dead community of Aquarius. They never knew.

IT WAS late afternoon on December 8.

They rolled over the hills, north of Tiburon, past the turnoff towards Corte Madera.

Now they were in a dead land, filled to overflowing with the urban corpses. The citizens of San Francisco, starving and beyond the edge of desperation, risking the barriers and armor of the National Guard and the state troopers, had tried to flee the catacombs of the city.

Time and again Mac had to ease the massive RV off the highways, squeezing past the rusting ruins of dozens of gridlocked cars and trucks.

It crossed his mind more than once that it might be better to abandon the Phantasm and stick to the jeep and the four-by-four. But they still faced an uncertain future, perhaps traveling on northward into the teeth of what might be a bitter winter. The shelter and comfort of the RV could easily mean the difference between surviving and dying.

Paul flashed his lights in the signal to halt, and Mac eased the vehicle over, avoiding a stalled Volvo station wagon with a snarling skeleton behind the wheel. The power brakes hissed on, and he switched off the engine and jumped down, aware of stiffness in his back and shoulders. He stretched to try to ease it a little. Behind the jeep he saw that Jeanne had pulled the four-by-four onto the hard shoulder.

"How much farther, Dad?"

"Only a few miles."

"Before dark?"

"Don't see why not."

Jeanne and Pamela had climbed out and joined them, while the two youngest children peered from the Phantasm, faces white blurs behind the windows, looking like little orphans locked away in an attic by a cruel stepmother.

"Can we rest up a day when we get to Muir Woods?" asked Jeanne. "Have to admit that I'm just starting to feel my age. This driving sure gets to you. So many poor devils lying dead, and nobody to give them Christian burial."

"We'll see when we get there. Might be nobody and nothing. Might be everybody and everything."

THERE WAS NOBODY, but there was a note. And a dry patch on the dark tarmac of the parking lot where Jim Hilton's vehicle had been parked throughout the days of snow.

The letter had been sealed in a clear plastic freezer bag, pinned securely to the main notice board right by the main entrance to the national monument.

"This is for Mac and Pete and Jeff and Nanci." It was dated that same day, the eighth.

"I'd forgotten he didn't know that poor old Pete bought the farm when those punks drilled him with the crossbow. Least he still thinks there's a chance that we're moving after him."

"Who's Nanci?" asked Jeanne McGill. "Somebody they picked up on the road?"

"Somebody the fragrant and gentle Jeff Thomas picked up, I guess." Mac shook his head, and went on reading aloud.

"We just met up with Kyle and Carrie. They have Steve's boy, Sly, with them. He's not too bright but a real good kid. Bad news for us all. Jed Herne's gone... died while traveling with Jeff. And Steve bought the farm a few days ago. Fell onto an electrified wire. Died quick. That's the best I can say. So, we're five now. If Mac gets this, I just realized he doesn't know that my wife and daughter Andrea died of what I reckon was cholera when I got home. Heather's with me, helping to keep me sane and on the straight and narrow."

"So much bloody dying," said Mac. "I sometimes think it might've been better if the *Aquila* had simply vaporized out in deep space."

Jeanne punched him hard on the upper arm. "For a bright guy you sure talk a lot of empty shit, McGill."

"No more real news from Zelig," Mac continued reading aloud.

"But it seems like this outfit, the Hunters of the Sun, is set against him and are also trying to find Aurora, which does seem to be the name of his base. Don't know much about the Hunters, except they got guns and money and appear to be organized. Watch out for them. We're talking some serious people here. Don't give out your real names to anybody suspicious, and likewise no mention of the good ship... They have a 'most wanted' list."

"They say where they've gone, Dad?" asked Jocelyn. "How old's Heather? She might be my friend."

"I'm our friend," protested Sukie.

"You mean *your* friend," said Pamela.

"Not my friend," argued the little girl, her face showing her stubborn confusion.

"Let it pass," said Mac, carrying on reading the last few lines of the handwritten note.

"Leaving now. Got two vehicles and enough gas to get us a few miles away up the coast. Still north is all I know, guys. Looked at the map and reckon we should be somewhere around Eureka the week before Christmas. I make it close to three hundred miles from here. Going to stay close to the Pacific when we can, on old Highway 1. That way we should miss any bad weather inland. Best I can suggest is we stay there for a couple of days, around December eighteenth. If anyone reads this, we'll see you. If Mac or anyone arrives later, I can only say to head on north. Hope to meet up one day. So long. Jim Hilton.''

They looked at one another, and Mac hauled out the dog-eared Rand McNally road atlas. ''Three hundred miles is about what I make it,'' said Paul McGill, looking over his father's shoulder.

''Could do that in a day, but things are not the same,'' said Mac. ''Time was we could have done that easily in a day. Breakfast at the coffee shop. Cinnamon rolls and coffee and eggs over easy or a big breakfast buffet. Stop off at a rest area for sandwiches and some fruit. Turkey sliced thin as tissue, then piled up thick, or a Reuben. Peaches with juice running down your chin. On through the afternoon, steady at fifty-five. Stop for gas and full-serve. Be in Eureka in time for a swim before dinner.''

''That was then, lover.'' Jeanne had tears glistening in her brown eyes.

''Sure. And this is now. I know which I prefer.''

They rested in Muir Woods for two whole days, recharging their batteries physically and mentally.

When they eventually set off toward the north again, they left the four-by-four behind them. Mac drove the Phantasm with Jeanne and the two younger girls. Paul and Pamela shared the responsibility for the jeep and the gas tank between them.

It was a beautiful dawn, with the sun rising away across the land, sending its lances of bright silver far over the expanse of the Pacific Ocean.

30

Gas was becoming a serious problem for the Hilton two-vehicle convoy as it picked its slow and careful way along the winding blacktop that had been Highway 1.

Jim's guesstimate as they left the relative security of Muir Woods had been that they had enough between them to travel about ninety to a hundred miles up the coast.

"Means we need to find some to syphon," said Carrie Princip. "Either go right down to the sea, or up inland. This area was kind of low on population, so there might be some around."

Kyle Lynch shook his head in disagreement. "Think about the floods of desperate refugees that came pouring out from San Francisco. They'd have drained everything dry. We'd be lucky if we find enough to ignite a mouse fart."

At first it looked as if the black ex-navigator of the *Aquila* might have been right.

The road was very congested for the first thirty or forty miles. Dozens of stalled vehicles, many of them still containing the withered corpses of their drivers, littered the way. It took them until well past noon to reach as far as Marshall, barely thirty miles north. Twice they had to take tortuous detours along dirt roads, even driving through the entrances to small farms and houses, cutting across the chewed-up remains of gardens and allotments.

Kyle was driving the second of the four-by-fours, with Carrie at his side. Sly Romero was sleeping contentedly in the back, snoring gently.

"This is like the moon, Carrie. Or some totally undiscovered planet out back of Alpha Centauri. Virtually no plant life left, except for a few patches of bright fresh moss among the dead crimson shrubs. Wish I had my camera with me. Next time we make a stop anywhere near a town, I might go look for one. Doubt that too many people looted cameras when the crunch came. I miss my photography as much as most things."

"Don't know what I miss most. I know that I missed my parents when that jackknifing son-of-a-bitch semi wiped them away up near Yellowstone. On their silver wedding anniversary yet. That was two years ago, but it seems like a whole lifetime away. I guess I miss simple things that are gone forever. Flopping out on a sofa with bare feet in front of a fire on a Sunday evening in winter, with a bag of sour cream-and-onion chips, watching the Saints beating the holy crap out of the Bears."

"I miss Daddy," came Sly's quiet voice from behind them, barely audible above the noise of the engine.

THEY'D JUST PASSED through Bodega Bay, where a skinny child had heaved a stone at Jim's truck, denting the side panel just below the window.

"Reckons that anyone driving has to be an enemy," said Heather, showing bland indifference to the brief attack.

"Guess so. Watch out. There's another one coming up, on your side."

"It's an old woman, Dad."

"So it is," he said, slowing down to a crawl, waving a hand out of the cab to warn Kyle.

It was bizarre. Here in the devastated wilderness of California was a neatly dressed elderly woman, apparently trying to hitch a ride.

Jim put on the brakes. "Stay here, Heather," he said. "I'll take a look."

The land on both sides of the road was clear of undergrowth and relatively flat. He didn't see how it could be an ambush. There had been plenty of better places for that within the past four or five miles.

The old lady was wearing a high-collared blouse with lace at the cuffs. A short quilted jacket was her only concession to the damp chill of the afternoon. A long skirt came down to midcalf, meeting the tops of her muddy black-buttoned boots. She had on what Jim could only think of as a bonnet with a cluster of multihued feathers stuck into its green ribbon. Her cheeks were a healthy pink, and she had on extremely thick glasses, making her watery blue eyes look gigantic.

"A good, good afternoon to you, young fellow. And the thanks of an old lady for your wonderful Christian charity in stopping. What a good Good Samaritan you are."

Her voice was light and trilling. Jim nodded. "Don't see many people trying to hitch a lift these days, ma'am."

"I found myself a little lost. Stupid when you realize that I've lived in these parts for fifty years." She sighed. "Fifty years and the world spinning around. Then the last year of red-scented damnation for us all."

"We can give you a ride."

"Bless you, my dear." Her silver hair was pulled back under the bonnet into a tight roll. Heavy amber earrings swung from side to side as she talked. "I believe that this is the highway north and south, is it not?"

Jim nodded. "Yeah. Which way do you want to go? Only we're getting kind of low on gas and it…"

"It isn't easy to get nowadays, is it. But I'll tell you what, Mr.... ?"

"Hilton, ma'am. Captain James Hilton."

"My name is Mercy Oliphaunt, Captain. I have plenty of gasoline in my garage back home. And you would be welcome to help yourself to all of it. Must be fifty gallons or more. I confess that I have always been something of a hoarder, but my little Metro was stolen in the first days after Earthblood so I have no use for it. A small reward for your kindness." She twinkled merrily at him. "And I have the makings for a lamb casserole in my larder. And an apple cobbler. I once won prizes at the county fair for my apple cobbler, Captain Hilton."

"You convinced me, Miss Oliphaunt."

She laid a gloved hand on his arm, as though she were a Southern belle being led into a summer ball, allowing him to escort her to the waiting truck. She happily squeezed in beside Heather Hilton.

"You must be the captain's pretty little daughter," she said brightly. "Remember, my dear child, that beliefs can be altered but the truth is inflexible and much, much more dangerous." She turned to Jim as he put the vehicle into gear again. "I was the teacher of our small community, Captain. I cannot resist trying to educate the young whenever I see them.''

"Which way, ma'am?"

"North. Then hang a right up a dirt road with a burned-out school bus just across the highway from it. Then it becomes a little more complex, and I will navigate for you. But we should be there in less than a half hour and eating before—'' she rolled up the cuff of her dress to consult a tiny gold watch ''—before five of the evening star.''

Heather Hilton caught a glimpse of a heavy scar around the wrist of the elderly woman, like a bracelet of wealed flesh. But it was gone so quickly that she couldn't really be sure she'd even seen it.

JIM STOOD BY THE VAN, listening to the ticking of the cooling engine. Dusk was creeping slowly toward them, bringing a light mist up from the direction of the sea. A westerly carried the scent of the ocean to him, though he was no longer sure quite how far away it was. Two or three times during the convoluted journey he'd begun to wonder if the delicate old lady weren't playing some kind of a trick on them as they wound up and down and left and right, along a trail that was often so narrow that the dead bushes scraped at both windows at once.

After they got to the spruce little cabin, Jim introduced Carrie, Kyle and Sly Romero to the old lady.

Carrie looked uncomfortable when Miss Oliphaunt looked her up and down.

Kyle shook the old lady's hand, which she extended as though she were bestowing some great favor on him.

Then Jim watched Miss Oliphaunt's face as she took a good look at Sly for the first time. She half turned toward him. "Oh, the poor child. Isn't he a...?"

"An orphan, ma'am," Jim completed swiftly. "Yeah, he is. Father got translated up into the realms eternal only a few days ago."

"Ah, yes," she said doubtfully. "He'll be all right inside the house, will he, Captain?"

"Be fine, will Sly. Won't you, son?"

"Me fine, Jim. Fine on line all mine."

At that Miss Oliphaunt nodded brightly, then went inside to get the meal ready for them and "to freshen up a little," explaining that she rarely had guests these days.

"LEAST SHE TOLD the truth about the gas. But she looked to be making a real effort not to wipe her fingers on her embroidered skirt after she shook hands with me. In case some of the black color had worn off on her ladylike skin." Kyle was rolling out one of the ten-gallon drums of fuel, while Sly and Jim were topping up the tanks of both the vehicles.

"Come on," said Carrie. "She's lonely and very old. Can't blame her if she still lives off politics that went out when Reagan finally handed in his boots and six-gun. Mind, she did make me feel like I was wearing dirty underwear."

A fluting voice from behind them made everyone turn around. "Food'll be on the table in five minutes. I assume you will all want to wash up."

"Yes, ma'am," replied Jim.

Heather grinned. "Was that a suggestion or a blued-steel order? I would've hated being in her class. Bet she used to hit the kids across the knuckles with the edge of a big ruler. If we're late, we'll all get detention."

They weren't late.

Jim had tried to paste down his thinning blond hair with water from a black-painted iron pump in the backyard. He had to agree with the others. Mercy Oliphaunt made him feel as if it was his first day in school.

The six-legged Colonial oak table was covered in a lace-edged muslin cloth so spotlessly white that it seemed to fill the room with its radiance. There were three gleaming brass lamps, two on a sideboard and one on a round table by the door to the dining room.

The cutlery looked as if it had just come, mint new, from its box, and Miss Oliphaunt had found time to hand-letter place cards for them all in a sloping italic script. Jim was to her left, with Carrie opposite him. Then Kyle and Sly, and Heather at the foot of the table.

"Would any of you wish to say grace?" she asked.

There was a shuffling of feet. Nobody wanted to meet those oddly huge eyes.

"Very well. After all, this is my humble demesne and I the chatelaine. It is seemly that the duty falls upon my frail shoulders."

Jim led the way, clasping his hands and dropping his eyes to the tabletop, glancing under lowered lids to make sure the others were following suit. Sly was last, looking around at everyone else. Then his face brightened, and he put his hands together and clamped his eyes tight shut.

Mercy Oliphaunt spoke. It struck Jim that the grace was not so much that of a humble supplicant to her Lord and Master but more an equal having a discussion about life.

"We are here, Jesus, ready to eat a fine meal. No doubt you helped provide some of the necessities, but I've done all the preparation and cooking. And

the big freezer out back is becoming woefully un-
derstocked, Jesus, so if you aim to assist me further, then it would be as well to get moving in that
direction." She raised her voice to include those
around her. "Thanks in the name of Father, Son
and Holy Ghost. Amen."

A ragged chorus of "Amens" followed, led by
Heather.

"Amen, Jesus, and I love you," came from Sly
Romero a few seconds later.

"Properly said, young man," said Mercy. "Now,
I shall go and bring in the repast. I trust all of you
have some fine and sturdy appetites?"

Not waiting for an answer, she swept out of the
dining room, her heels clicking along the passage
toward the kitchen.

Kyle grinned at the others. "Anyone who looks
like an adman's ideal of the American granny has
to cook like a dream. Lamb casserole and apple
cobbler."

Carrie licked her lips. "Boy, oh boy. You realize
that we haven't had a *real* old-fashioned meal since
the *Aquila* came down at Stevenson?"

Jim nodded. "That's true. Hey, Heather, why
not go see if Miss Oliphaunt needs a hand out
there?"

"Sure."

Sly was looking worried, and Kyle leaned toward him, grinning. "Cheer up. What's wrong?"

"Well, Kyle, me think Dad is seeing and looking and watching me."

"Yeah?"

"So, if me eat lots of apple cobbler will Dad be real angry with Sly?"

"No, of course not. Chances to stoke up the engines are few and far between, Sly. Eat as much as you want." Kyle hesitated. "Just don't make yourself sick."

Heather reappeared and sat down. "Says she doesn't need help. Only be a minute."

"You see the food?" asked Carrie.

The girl bit her lip. "Yeah. Well, kind of."

Her father frowned. "Now what does...? Doesn't matter. I hear her coming."

Kyle rubbed his hands together. "I tell you, friends. This is going to be one meal to remember."

31

Nanci Simms was very good indeed at inflicting pain.

Good at knowing precisely where the limits were between simply making a man weep and reducing him to the state where he would lose all control of his body and slip away into the dark wilderness of unconsciousness.

If that happened, then it was no fun.

No fun to flog a dead horse, as one of Nanci's CIA instructors had often told her, back around the year 2025, at one of those anonymous mansions that used to lie in the green valleys of West Virginia.

Her reasons for keeping Jeff Thomas alive were purely selfish. In any other situation, the way he'd left her to die alone from the severed artery in her thigh would have merited death. As long and slow as time would allow.

Despite his self-serving cowardice, resembling a trapped sewer rat, Nanci was experienced enough in survivalism to know that the chances of living in post-Earthblood America were considerably enhanced if you had someone there to watch your back every now and again.

Granted, you might also need to watch your back against that very person some of the time. But it was still a reasonable trade-off. And she had done what she could to discourage Jeff Thomas from ever betraying her again.

An extra consideration in her careful, clinical punishment was that she knew well enough that she was dealing with a man who was a serious sexual masochist. Someone who would relish abasing himself by licking her boots while she whipped him. Who would grovel in the dirt, begging for greater and greater humiliations at the hands of his dominant mistress. At the hands, and other parts of her lean, tanned body.

Nanci knew the feeling, knew it from the other edge of the same sword. For her there was overwhelming sexual fulfillment in having someone like Jeff helpless beneath her. The fact that it was all a kind of morbid game didn't diminish the flooding delight that surged through her as she dragged him down into ever-deeper levels of perverse degradation.

But this time, while they waited together in the darkness to complete their escape, had been different. The lesson had to be forced home into Jeff's mind. A lesson that made clear the distinction between pain and pleasure.

Once, as the searching helicopter from the Hunters of the Sun flooded the barren hillside ten miles away with its futile searchlight, Nanci recalled the oldest of all jokes about the sadomasochistic relationship.

"Hit me, hit me," begged the masochist.

"No," smiled the sadist.

It had been like that. His pale bruised body, naked on the harsh pebbles, his ankles tied together, hands bound in the small of his back. A cord from his wrists around his neck, tight enough to make his breathing difficult, but not quite tight enough to throttle him.

Nanci had begun by making Jeff relax, cleverly allowing him the space to enjoy the start of the familiar games. It was all very gentle.

Then she changed the rules.

Upped the ante.

Using every splinter of her considerable sexual skills to bring him to the brink of a rushing satisfaction, then withholding that delight. Gradually working in a little more serious pain.

"Now the good times stop, Jefferson," she whispered. "Out here in the desert you can scream and scream until your throat turns bleeding raw. And there isn't anyone to hear you. Chopper's gone back to base. Hours to dawn. You and me. Think what you might be like by then. Think on what you did to me, Jefferson.

"The next hour's going to be unrelieved suffering, Jefferson, while you pay me my blood price. Then . . . then I'll decide on what to do with you. Decide if I can maybe trust you one more time. Can I?"

There was a desperate, choking mumble that she took to be assent.

"Cord a little tight around your neck, Jefferson? Never mind. Least I haven't gagged you. Reason is that you enjoy that part. That isn't what this is about, dear boy. Now, let's carry on with this lesson a while longer."

Finally, with the first fingers of rosy light peering over the distant hills to the east, Nanci Simms relented. Gave him life instead of death.

Gave herself the pleasure that she'd kept under simmering control and even allowed Jeff Thomas the relief that his tortured body had been seeking.

ODDLY the betrayal and subsequent punishment seemed to bind them closer together.

As they headed north and west, moving at the fastest speed they could manage, Jeff was like a new puppy fawning on his adored new owner.

But deep inside his soul there burned a tiny flickering ruby of irredeemable hatred for the older woman. For what she had done to him out in the darkness. Something that he would never quite forget. Never quite forgive.

It didn't show, Jeff knew, not on his face, not in his voice. But when he'd catch her shrewd eyes once in a while, he felt deep down that without a doubt she knew.

Their drive toward the late rendezvous at Muir Woods was relatively uneventful, except for the roadblock they encountered around noon on the first day. Four men and a woman, well dressed and well armed, flagged them down from behind a couple of flatbed trucks. The fields around were barren, covered in a thin blanket of soiled, melting snow.

Nanci had slowed the four-by-four, smiling at the group through the muddied windshield but talking to Jeff out of the corner of her mouth.

"Keep your .38 in your lap. Don't even try and move until I open fire. Then come out the door as fast as you can and try and take out anyone that I miss."

There wasn't time to argue with her, not even a moment to ask why couldn't they turn around and drive quickly away in the opposite direction.

But Nanci answered the unspoken question as she eased on the brakes around thirty yards from the armed band. "They got gas and food and we don't, Jeff."

The folks behind the block hadn't seen anyone trying to pass through their community in several days. There had been the first rush after the full horror of Earthblood was revealed, followed by the brief period when the authorities attempted to prevent travel in order to minimize and localize the catastrophe. Then the torrent of refugees streamed from the towns and cities.

The fighting and killing had been desperate, and a number of their friends and relations had died defending their inalienable right to bear arms and use them to keep all outlanders from their doors.

Nowadays the torrent had fallen below a trickle. The four-by-four was only of minimal interest. They had the guns and they could see there were only a couple of strangers in the cab.

It wasn't likely to be a problem.

Nanci deliberately didn't try to hide the Port Royale machine pistol as she climbed slowly and painfully down. She held it loose, dangling down in her left hand, trying to make it appear no sort of threat.

"Hi, there. Name's Veronica Poole. Retired teacher from Fort Worth. This is my brother's boy, Jeff. We had hard times coming, friends."

They saw a stooped, frail, retired schoolmarm walking toward them and hardly noticed the powerful gun that dropped from her hand. Before any of them had really registered what she was doing, Nanci was less than five yards from them, smiling hesitantly.

"Wonder if we might beg a cup of water," she said.

Henry Harrison was in charge of the roadblock. A retired accountant, he had been one of the leading voices for withdrawing their patrols. He'd relied on critical-path analysis and flow charts to explain that the statistics showed they were no longer needed and that their isolated hamlet could now be protected in far more efficient ways, utilizing less time and manpower.

But the self-protection committee had decided by a small majority that they would maintain the patrol for another few days, until Christmas, then review the situation again before the New Year.

Henry watched the elegantly dressed old woman as she walked toward them, setting each foot carefully in front of the other as though she had some sort of crippling knee or hip condition. It crossed his mind that she might be a doctor. They didn't have anyone with real medical training and they'd agreed unanimously that if a doctor or even a nurse happened to turn up, they'd be invited to stay.

His mouth was already open to warn the stranger not to get close, when he realized with a start that she was already very close. Asking them something about letting her have some water.

"That's about—" began Henry, holding up his hand self-importantly.

"Far enough?" said Nanci Simms, her smile unchangingly bright and friendly.

It stayed friendly even as she squeezed the trigger on the Port Royale, on full-auto.

At the harsh, snarling cough of the machine pistol, Jeff Thomas rolled quickly out of the passenger's door, the unfamiliar .38 in his hand.

He managed a clumsy somersault and came up in something approximating the gunfighter's crouch that Nanci had managed to teach him.

Finger white on the spur trigger, he was looking for someone to shoot, but he saw only four men and one woman, all of them already in various stages of dying.

Henry Harrison got the first three rounds, each of the 9 mm rounds hitting him in less than a quarter of a second, all of them within an inch of his breastbone. The impact sent him staggering backward, almost running, before he tripped over his own feet.

Strangely his last coherent thought was disappointment that the elderly woman wasn't a doctor after all.

His friends to left and right were shot at close range, all between throat and stomach, each one taking a 3-round burst of lead.

Nanci was skilled enough to control the spitting machine pistol, making sure that she had a single round left if any of her victims needed it. And there was always the P-111 automatic in the back of her belt. But her ability was such that she didn't need to fire again.

"Judas on the tree!" exclaimed Jeff Thomas, rising cautiously from the crouch. He'd already dismissed as stillborn the tempting but transient idea that he should try to shoot Nanci in the back while he had a half chance, realizing that half a chance wasn't anywhere near to good enough.

"Gas and food, Jefferson," she said.

Within eighty seconds all of the five were finally still. One of them had carried on writhing and gurgling and bleeding longer than the others.

Jeff holstered his .38 and began the task of syphoning fuel from the two flatbed trucks into their own vehicle, while Nanci searched the corpses for anything worth the stealing. She found nothing beyond some extra ammunition for her two guns. Reloading the Port Royale, she waited for Jeff to finish refueling.

"Any spare cans, take them and fill them," she said. "I'll see what these friendly folk might have to offer us in the way of sustenance."

There was bread, only slightly stale, and enough jerked beef to last the two of them a week. Half a pecan pie, which she ate without even offering any to Jeff, and three cans of cling peaches in raspberry nectar.

"Better than nothing. How are we for gas?"

"Tank's full," he said, spitting in the dirt what he'd accidentally sucked into his mouth. "And there's about seven gallons spare in the back."

"Good. They got some decent Mexican bottled beer in the cab of one of their trucks. Help yourself. It'll get the taste of the gas away."

"Are we going in to their township?"

"Why?"

"Might be more food and gas."

"Why?"

"Well, we can't have too much. Can we, Nanci?"

"Yeah, we can. What we want is always to try and keep just that little more than we need. Now, have that beer and we'll get moving. Should reach Muir Woods easily tomorrow."

They camped overnight less than ten miles from their destination.

Jeff had wanted to press on, but Nanci pointed out there was no point in trying to drive after dark. Not with coiling mists coming ghosting in off the Pacific close by.

IT WAS a beautiful dawn, with the sun rising away to their right and behind them.

Jeff was at the wheel. The blacktop snaked around, occasionally allowing glimpses of it a mile or so ahead, and lower down. They were both surprised to see that the plant cancer didn't appear to have touched some of the big redwoods that they could now make out in the bright morning light.

"Too big," commented the woman. She was sitting with her feet on the dash, holding the Port Royale across her lap. Jeff had been allowed to make love to her the night before, and there was a friendly atmosphere between them, more like a contented and long-married couple.

The Pacific was visible to their left, over the rolling gullies, and Jeff pulled over and stopped, switching off the engine. "Now, that is really beautiful," he said.

Nanci leaned out of her window and took a deep breath. Her whole body suddenly stiffened. "What's that? Someone's coming, Jefferson.

There! Just spotted it. Should make that plural, though. Big RV and a four-by-four towing a trailer. Now that's the way to travel."

"What're we going to do?"

She was outside, all action, like a hungry panther. "Park this a quarter-mile back where the road dips. I'll ambush whoever it is, and we'll be driving in comfort and style."

"Be careful."

She grinned and patted him on the cheek. "Don't worry, Jefferson. Be like candy from a baby."

Now he could hear the deep rumble of the large camper's engine as it drove up the switchback hills toward them in a low gear. Nanci put a finger and thumb together and grinned at him. She ran with an athletic ease that he envied toward a bunch of dead sycamores that fronted the road.

Jeff quickly swung the four-by-four around and went to park it where she'd told him. He'd had only the barest glimpse of the lead vehicle in the distance, but he thought it was the model called a Phantasm. Some cousin of his father from up in New Hampshire had once come down to San Luis Obispo to visit in one of them. It had a microwave and freezer and cooker and all the conveniences money could buy. Including a big double bed.

Jeff liked the idea of that double bed.

He left the four-by-four, locking it carefully, and started to run along the blacktop back to rejoin Nanci, his .38 drawn and ready.

But the morning stillness was broken by the sound of the Port Royale being fired, the noise sending a flock of red-capped jays squawking into the cloudless sky.

"Shit," he said. "Too late again."

32

The lamb casserole was in a large lidded ovenproof dish that Miss Oliphaunt carried in to them, wearing pretty floral kitchen gloves. Her face was flushed, and steam was condensing on the thick lenses of her glasses.

She was panting a little as she rested the food on a mat at the center of the table. "There! Goodness, but I'm not getting any younger."

"None of us are," said Jim gallantly.

"I'll go and bring in the apple cobbler. But you folks make a start tucking into the main course. Take care not to burn your tongues."

She was gone before it registered on any of them just what she'd said. Kyle broke the silence. "Why's she bringing in dessert before we start the casserole?"

"Search me." Jim turned to look out through the door, but he couldn't see into the kitchen. "Best get started on this, I guess." He reached out for the lid of the casserole, then realized that it was likely to be scaldingly hot. He picked up his linen napkin to protect his fingers.

"Dad," Heather said, her voice sharp.

"What?"

"I saw what . . . something really weird."

"Tell me. Come on, quick. Before she comes back in with the apple cobbler."

Heather reached and laid her hand flat on top of the oven dish before anyone could stop her. Leaning forward, half-out of her seat, she looked around at the others. "See. That's it. Cold as a stone."

Carrie stood up. "Then what's inside . . . ?" She let the words trail off as she lifted the lid. "Oh, shit."

She tilted the casserole, showing it to everyone around the table.

It was lamb, all right.

The head of a lamb.

Eyes and wool and mud and teeth and all.

Raw and bloody, sinews and gristle showing where it had recently been hacked from a carcass, it was surrounded by uncooked, unwashed vegetables. Half a dozen slug-eaten carrots and some unshelled peas with a handful of green, moldy potatoes were all swilling about in several inches of pink, scummy, cold water.

"Horrid and ugly," said Sly Romero, his voice hardly even a whisper.

"Yeah," agreed Jim Hilton.

Lulled by the comfortable cottage and the chintzy cheeriness of Mercy Oliphaunt, he was slow to react to the revelation of the bizarre meal and was still sitting when the elderly lady came back into the room.

"Apples are still a'growing," she crowed in her high, quavery voice. Then something flashed in her hand, and she was trying to get close to Heather— close enough to hack her neck with a bone-handled, serrated carving knife.

The girl screamed and ducked away to her left, falling off her chair. Sly also screamed, thin and piercing, like a stallion at the gelding. He tried to stand up to go to Heather's aid, but slipped and fell over backward, banging his head on the polished wooden floor.

Both Carrie and Kyle had hung their coats out in the hall, her Smith & Wesson .22 and his .32-caliber Mondadori automatic in the pockets.

Jim was the only one armed, the powerful Ruger revolver on his right hip. But he was taken by surprise, stunned by the sudden violence of the attack on his daughter.

Mercy Oliphaunt was yelping with crazed laughter, with the terrifying echo of a rabid coyote, her staring eyes like glazed pinwheels, flailing with the knife at the young girl who'd managed to scramble her way out of reach beneath the table.

"Little piggies come to fucking supper!" Realizing that she couldn't get at the girl, the old woman turned toward her paralyzed father. "Cook the fattest piggy first," she whooped, her voice triumphant, and her whole body suddenly infused with a wild energy.

Finally the ice melted from Jim's brain and muscles, and he reacted. He reached up with a serving spoon in his left hand to parry the vicious knife in a flurry of sparks, simultaneously sliding out of his seat, right hand clawing for the heavy .44.

The neat little dining room was brimming over with panic, everyone trying to do what seemed best.

From under the table, Heather was watching for the button boots, aiming to keep the width of the table between herself and the homicidal crone.

Sly was kicking his feet in the air like an overturned beetle, great gobbets of tears coursing down his chubby cheeks as he struggled to regain his balance.

Carrie threw the casserole at Mercy Oliphaunt, and the severed head of the lamb hit the woman a glancing blow on the shoulder, the greasy, bloodied water staining her blouse.

Kyle Lynch had grabbed up a pair of knives from the table and was beginning to move cautiously around toward their attacker.

But Miss Oliphaunt seemed totally oblivious to any threat toward herself, laughing and sawing at the air with the glittering blade while Jim tried to fend her off and pull the stubborn Ruger from its holster.

"Fuck off," he snarled, feeling like someone trapped in the nightmare where a nameless, shapeless creature pursues you along an endless corridor. And your feet are snared in molasses as it comes closer and closer, until you run out of corridor.

"Join all my little children," she said, her voice now shockingly calm and reasonable.

The gun felt heavier than he remembered as it finally came free. Thirty-five ounces, six-inch barrel. Six rounds of .44 full metal jacket. Full-length ejector shroud, cushioned grips with walnut inserts.

Facts. Cold facts.

Not like a genteel schoolteacher with mad eyes, attacking you with a carving knife in the middle of her own dining room.

Think about that, and you found yourself wandering along the meandering path toward insanity.

Facts. Stick to facts.

Wide trigger. The smooth action and the deep-set, checkered hammer clicking back.

Mercy Oliphaunt made an instant change of tactics as she saw the blued-steel revolver in the hand of her intended victim, showing a moment of cunning sanity as she ducked away and lunged toward the helpless teenage boy.

Jim had a splinter of a second to alter his aim and snap off a shot at the moving target.

"Missed me, Beelzebub!" she giggled in delight as she disappeared behind the table.

"Stop her, Daddy!" Sly's voice almost unrecognizable in the depths of terror.

Jim dropped to his knees, but he snagged the tablecloth and pulled it half off the table, cutlery and china and glasses clattering and shattering on the floor, making it impossible to see clearly enough to try for a second shot.

There was a strange sound amid the chaos, a noise that managed to be both dull and sharp at the same time.

"You wicked slattern," said Mercy Oliphaunt, sounding just as if she'd caught one of her pupils writing obscenities on the outhouse wall.

"I stabbed her, Dad," Heather said, a tremble in her voice that mixed fear and exultation.

Now Jim could see what was going on.

Sly had his knees drawn up to his chin and was waving his hands in front of his staring eyes.

Heather, backing away toward the far side of the table, was crawling through the detritus of the nightmare meal toward Carrie and Kyle.

And there was Mercy Oliphaunt, face twisted in a rictus of grinning hatred, kneeling in the shadows. The steel carving blade was still gripped tightly in her right hand, twitching as though it had been connected to a high-voltage wire.

The hilt of a butter knife stuck out of her left eye, behind the distorting glasses, like some obscene piece of jewelry. Blood, mingled with clear, aqueous fluid, leaked from the blinded orb.

"Tried to take my little ones away. School comes first." She crawled very slowly toward Jim Hilton. "I stopped that nonsense for good and all."

"Shoot her, Dad."

Heather's voice broke the hypnotic spell that had gripped Jim, turning him into a helpless rabbit in front of the weaving coils of a rattler.

The wide trigger came back once.

His hand jerked upward, the roar deafening under the long table, with a blur of smoke from the explosion.

The .44 almost ripped the old woman's head clear off her scrawny shoulders. The bullet struck her through the bridge of her beaky nose, angling upward and exiting through the top of the table, smashing into the white-painted ceiling. It lifted the top of her cranium, splattering the floor with blood and brains and matted silvery hair.

Her glasses flew off, landing right by Jim's knee, the thick lenses slobbered with a gray-pink grue.

"It's all right, Sly," Jim said, trying to keep his voice steady and reassuring. "It's over."

When they had calmed down a little, they dragged the limp corpse outside and tidied up the dining room, restoring things to normal. Heather, Sly and Kyle went out into the tidy little kitchen to start cooking up something approximating a proper meal.

They'd agreed that it would be foolish to leave such a secure place, when there was warmth and shelter, but that they'd move on north first thing in the morning.

"At least we got some gas, and there's quite a cache of canned meat and fruit in the larder." Carrie was still pale from the effects of the horrific scene. "Won't be sorry to get out and back into the clean air. Got the feeling that she might rise up like one of the walking dead and come after me in the darkness."

She and Jim were alone together in the hall, with framed steel engravings of European mountains frowning grimly down from both the walls.

He put his arm around her. "Want to stay the night with me, Carrie?" he asked.

"Yeah. Think I would. Not for...you know. Just to get me some warm vibes from you."

HE WENT UP the narrow staircase to check out the sleeping arrangements. Mercy's own room was neat, with a dimity nightgown laid over the end of the double bed. Two guest rooms each had single beds. And then in the attic, two small rooms had been knocked through into one.

He'd thought it was over, but now he realized they hadn't known all.

"Oh, Christ," he breathed, understanding now the old woman's runic comments about not allowing them to take her pupils away from her.

The attic had been turned into a classroom, complete with seven mummified little corpses leaning crookedly in three rows of tiny desks, facing a blackboard. On it, in the same old-fashioned and elegant hand, was chalked a single sentence.

"All work and no play makes Jack a dull boy."

Jim closed the door very quietly and went back down the stairs to tell the others.

33

Nanci Simms had found the ideal position for her ambush on a bank overlooking the blacktop, behind a fringe of dead huckleberries, with a forest of sturdy redwoods at her back. She could take out the driver and anyone in the cab of the lumbering Phantasm RV as they drew level with her. There were metal guards on both sides of the highway, so it wouldn't topple over the cliff. By the time the driver of the jeep towing the fuel tank realized what was happening, she'd have killed him with a second burst of fire from the stubby machine pistol.

The leading vehicle was less than two hundred yards away, moving little faster than walking speed. The sunlight reflected off the shield made it impossible to see who was driving. But that wasn't a problem for Nanci Simms.

It wasn't likely to be anyone she knew.

As she crouched and waited, it crossed Nanci's mind that most people that she'd ever known well had died . . . and most of them she'd killed herself.

The noise of the RV was deafening. For a moment she thought that she caught the sound of movement behind her, among the sun-dappled shadows beneath the sweeping branches. She turned and stared but couldn't spot anything moving.

The Phantasm was around a hundred yards away, then fifty, moving even more slowly as it neared the crest of the rise.

Then the range was down to thirty yards.

She brought the gun up to her shoulder, ready to open fire as the woods seemed to be trembling with the roaring of the engine.

One of Nanci's many attributes was peripheral vision over twenty percent better than what used to be the national average. Out of the corner of her right eye she caught the faintest flicker of movement and started to spin around.

The trio of dogs were less than twenty feet away, charging at her, bellies down, hunting in a menacing silence. There was a moment to place them as some mix of German shepherd and rottweiler, then she pulled the trigger.

The burst of lead from the Port Royale ripped the animals apart, slaughtering all three of them instantly. But the center dog was already in midair, committed to its leap for the woman's throat, fangs bared.

It struck Nanci on the chest, knocking the gun from her hands and sending her staggering backward. Tripping over an exposed root of one of the redwoods, she slithered through the brittle fronds of the huckleberries, rolling down the slope, pushing away the snarling corpse, dust blinding her.

The rotting stump of a dead aspen brought Nanci to a sudden, jolting stop, hitting her under the ribs, driving all the breath from her body.

She was aware through the breathless pain that the Phantasm had stopped and that one of the doors had opened. Boots stopped close to her, and there was a mutter of voices, but the idling engine was way too loud for her to hear the words. Farther off came the faint echo of someone running.

Then the click of a gun's hammer being cocked.

So, she thought. This is how it ends. A sunlit road in the country.

Could be worse ways to go.

JEFF HAD BEGUN running back down the narrow, twisting road as soon as he heard the sound of the Port Royale spitting out its full-auto load of death. His own .38 was ready in his hand, though his time with Nanci Simms made him certain that his own contribution wasn't likely to be needed.

When he sprinted over the crown of the next steep hill, he found himself staring down onto a bizarre and totally inexplicable tableau.

There was a dead or dying animal, thrashing and squealing on the edge of the pavement, so smeared in blood it was impossible to tell what it might once have been. A pig or a small deer, was Jeff's blind guess.

The cream-and-brown Phantasm had stopped, its exhaust smoking a little, the driver's door swinging open. Behind it, just visible, was the jeep, with a tall, bearded man getting out, holding a pump-action shotgun.

Lying still in the dirt, her khaki suit covered in dust, was the unmistakable figure of Nanci Simms, the machine pistol glittering in the sunlight a couple of feet away from her outstretched hand.

But the person dominating the scene was a heavily built, muscular man with grizzled hair. He was holding a shotgun, barrel pointing down toward Nanci.

The man started to turn toward Jeff as he heard the sound of the pounding boots on the tarmac.

Something about him brought Jeff to a dead halt. He stared for a second, then started to yell at the top of his lungs.

"Mac! Holy shit, Mac! It's me. Don't shoot, Mac, it's me. It's me!"

Nanci, fighting for breath, was beginning to re-cover a little. She was aware of the shouts and the voice of the man who held the 16-gauge Brazzi scattergun aimed at her. She noticed the tone of surprise, tinged with something that remarkably resembled disgust.

"Well, I'll go to the top of our stairs, folks. If it's not Jeff Thomas."

JEANNE McGILL had copied out the original note from Jim Hilton and she showed it to Jeff and Nanci as they all sat together in the living area of the Phantasm. Introductions had been made, and everyone was sharing mugs of instant decaf and a plate of chocolate-chip cookies.

Mac was watching Jeff while he read the note, sitting on the sofa with Nanci Simms at his side.

There was something about the ex-journalist that had always gotten on Henderson McGill's nerves. An arrogance that was somehow underlaid with a strange subservience, as though he was equally ready to hit out at you or be hit himself and didn't care all that much which it was.

Nanci had recovered from the shock of the at-tack by the dogs and had used the RV facilities to wash and clean herself, helped by Jeanne and Pa-mela. Mac was equally uneasy about their new companion. Retired schoolteacher from Fort

Worth, she'd said. Though she didn't flaunt herself, he knew enough about bodybuilding and weight training to recognize someone who was in terrific shape despite admitting to being around the middle fifties.

But company was company. And Nanci certainly looked like someone who would handle herself well in any emergency, and life after Earthblood was one emergency after another.

Jeff laid down the piece of paper, half closing his eyes as he did his arithmetic. "How many of the old *Aquila* left, then? Only five? Is that right?"

Mac nodded. "Looks like it. You and me. Jim and Carrie and Kyle Lynch."

Jeff whistled. "High mortality."

"Not so high as throughout the country," said Nanci. "My guess is that there's a lot less than one left alive from every five hundred."

Paul McGill nodded, carefully putting down his empty mug on a shelf. "From what we've seen driving from New England, Miss Simms, it could be even worse than that."

"Difficult to tell, though." Pamela McGill looked at her father. "We supposed there's quite a few taken to the back country and just plain vanished."

Mac glanced toward his first wife. "Any chance of a refill, Jeanne? Thanks. Yeah, Pamela, there could be dozens within a hundred yards as you drive by."

Nanci Simms leaned back, wincing as she felt the bruising under her ribs. "Whoa, that bastard dog nearly did me some serious damage. Like they used to say about the Apaches, Mac . . . if you could see them then they were there. And if you couldn't see them, then they were *really* there."

"How about this place—" Jeff consulted the note again "—Eureka? We going there?" As he waited for Mac to reply, he added, "You were heading south?"

"That's the way out from Muir Woods that's open. Then we cut back and head north."

"We got some good maps." Jocelyn and Sukie had been shy of the two strangers, hiding out in the kitchen, peering around the edge of the door. Now the older of the girls was confident enough to show Nanci and Jeff a big Rand McNally atlas.

"We also got them state by state," said Pamela. "And some hiking-scale ones."

"Got them for this area of Northern California?" asked Nanci. "Though I reckon I know these parts fairly well. Used to hike and backpack a lot when I was younger. I fear I'm past all that now."

Mac was watching Jeff Thomas as she said this and he caught the cynical grin, quickly masked, that flitted across the badly scarred face.

"You know Eureka?" asked Jeanne. "Sounds like an exciting sort of a name."

Nanci smiled. "Only time I was there it was cold and wet and a fog in off the water. Maybe I was unlucky." She studied the copy of the note again. "What does he mean about this boy, Sly, not being too bright. Do I detect a subtext there, Mac?"

"Sort of. Lad's got Down's syndrome. Steve coped well, but it never sat right with his ex-wife. What was her name? Alice? No. Alison, that was it. Took to drink over the boy. Broke their marriage."

Nanci tutted her disapproval. "Might be that this Sly doesn't see all of the things that we do. Then again, I'll bet you that he sees some things that we don't."

Mac saw his own ex-wife and his children nod at what the older woman had said. It showed her wisdom and made it easier for her to be accepted into their group. But he was more cynical. From what he knew, it was obvious that Jeff and Nanci had already met Sly Romero. So she'd know all about him. But the others hadn't noticed the trick.

He decided that Nanci Simms merited some careful watching.

Jeff had taken the note. "Three hundred miles up the coast. That going to be the best route?"

Paul McGill answered him. "We spent some time on the maps, Jeff. There are other possibilities, cutting inland. But if Jim Hilton's going to try that way, then we might as well do the same. We got a couple of days less than him."

"December 18," said Nanci. "Shouldn't be that hard. You got fuel?"

"Enough for that," said Pamela. "But not a whole lot to get us farther."

"Cross that bridge when we reach it." She looked at Jeanne. "Any more coffee?"

THE FOUR-BY-FOUR went out in front, Nanci at the wheel. Mac drove the Phantasm carefully along the treacherously narrow and winding roads, with Paul bringing up the rear towing the fuel truck, Pamela at his side. Jeanne and the two youngest children were in the rear of the RV.

They'd barely started, just past the turnoff to Bolinas, when they saw the sign.

Nanci braked, holding her hand out of the window in the agreed signal for them to stop. Everyone got down, staring at the weather-stained billboard.

It had originally advertised Acme Coyote Traps. The slogan beneath the picture of a ravenous animal slavering over the mangled corpse of a sheep said Get Your Retaliation In First. Do It To Him With An Acme Coyote Trap.

But that wasn't what had caught Nanci's eye.

It had been the painted graffiti on the billboard, done so crudely that it would have been passed by without a second glance by anyone driving Highway 1.

A daubed block of maroon, the color streaked, gobbets running down, puddled in the dirt. The paint formed a rough circle with a series of small silver-white blobs.

"It's the space-mission flag," said Henderson McGill. "By God, but it is. A circle of silver stars on a background of maroon. Who put it there and what does . . . ?"

The recent bad weather had damaged the big billboard, leaving some of the advertisement hanging in ragged strips and making it difficult to read the message that had been scrawled in the same red paint.

"North is right. On the way to AR."

And underneath that was a rough zigzag. Like the mark of Zorro.

"Zelig," breathed Jeff Thomas. "Aurora really does exist, then."

"Oh, yeah," agreed Nanci. "Never doubted it. Nor do the Hunters of the Sun."

"The who?" asked Jeanne McGill.

"Long story, my dear. Let's get our convoy back into gear and then, perhaps tonight, around a bright camp fire, I'll tell you what there is to be known." Nanci turned and strode toward the four-by-four, Jeff trailing obediently after her.

As he climbed into the Phantasm, Mac wondered quite how this retired teacher from Texas came to know quite so much about General Zelig.

But that could wait on the back burner.

The three vehicles began to move north again through the December sunshine.

Free-lance talent from the crumbling
Russian Empire fuels Iraq's
nuclear power in

DON PENDLETON'S
MACK BOLAN®

STONY MAN™ 9
STRIKEPOINT

With a combination of state-of-the-art technology, weapons
and combat skills, the Stony Man team—
Mack Bolan, Able Team and Phoenix Force—
battles the enemies of civilized man in a quest across
Europe, knowing that a single misstep means disaster
for the world.

GOLD
EAGLE

SM9

BATTLE FOR THE FUTURE IN A WASTELAND OF DESPAIR

AURORA QUEST

by JAMES AXLER

The popular author of DEATHLANDS® brings you the gripping conclusion of the Earthblood trilogy with AURORA QUEST. The crew of the U.S. space vessel *Aquila* returns from a deep-space mission to find that a devastating plant blight has stripped away all civilization.

In what's left of the world, the astronauts grimly cling to a glimmer of promise for a new start.

Available in July at your favorite retail outlet.

Are you looking for more

DEATHLANDS®

by JAMES AXLER

Don't miss these stories by one of
Gold Eagle's most popular authors: